THE
DESPERATE
RIDERS

Also by Lee Martin

Shadow on the Mesa
Fast Ride to Boot Hill
The Last Wild Ride
The Grant Conspiracy: Wake of the Civil War
Fury at Cross Creek
In Mysterious Ways
Revenge at Rawhide
The Maverick Gun
Fury at Sweetwater Pass
The Lone Rider
Black River
Dead Man's Trail
Valley of the Lawless
Track the Men Down
The Danger Trail
Hang Town
Dead Man's Creek
Ride the Wild Wind
The Siege at Rhyker's Station

The Darringer Brothers Series:

Trail of the Fast Gun
Trail of the Long Riders
Trail of the Hunter
Trail of the Circle Star
Trail of the Restless Gun
Trail of the Dangerous Gun

THE DESPERATE RIDERS

LEE MARTIN

Vaca Mountain Press
Vacaville, California, U.S.A.

Vaca Mountain Press
Paperback ISBN 13: 978-1-952380-66-2
Kindle ISBN 13: 978-1-952380-67-9

Also available in:
Large Print Paperback ISBN 13: 978-1-952380-68-6

Cover and interior design by Deirdre Wait, High Pines Creative
Cover images © Getty Images

Published by Vaca Mountain Press
Vacaville, California, U.S.A.

Visit Lee Martin Westerns on Facebook.

*To my wonderful family and
in memory of my beautiful sister Arlene,
our beloved mother, our rough riding brothers,
and for Jim Liontas.*

CHAPTER ONE

In spring of 1878, in northeastern Colorado's open country, golden in the sun, lay the small cowtown of Two Wells. North of the weatherbeaten town, a creaky windmill, its silver blades peppered with bullet holes, slowly turned in a rising breeze. Next to it stood a long watering trough and corrals. Beyond was the livery, a banging shutter hanging from the front window.

With a dusty main street, one saloon, the office of the county sheriff, a few stores, and a boarding house, it only came to life on Saturday nights, when ranch hands came for as good a time as the sleepy town might allow.

On one lazy and sunny Friday afternoon that was about to explode in violence, a single farm wagon hauling a load of hay was passing through, stirring up red dust in the sunlight as it headed for the livery. An old man with a full white beard slept on a bench in the shade next to the general store, while hats and boots hung overhead under the eaves. Horses stood quiet at the hitching rails. A little black dog chased something under the boardwalk.

Purchasing shells inside the cluttered general store, Kansas Red, thirty-seven years old, had always been a mystery. Known only as a deadly gunfighter and sometimes bounty hunter, he could also quote from the Bible at any time. His face was haunted and lean with cold, blue eyes. His thick, shoulder-length hair, thin mustache, and trim beard were dark brown with an auburn tint.

Dressed all in black with a leather vest and wide brimmed hat, Kansas carried his Army Colt in a cutaway, tied-down holster on his right hip. His bandana was dark red and loose. No one ever dared ask him who he really was or if he was even from Kansas.

In the back of the store, two middle-aged women were looking at yellow ribbons on a table, out of earshot.

Up front and behind the counter, handing Kansas boxes of .44 shells and other items in a sack, Red Linstrom, the ever-friendly store keeper—fifty-five with a nicely-trimmed grey beard, and sporting a striped vest—cautioned him in a hush.

"The kid's hardly sixteen or seventeen, wears a strapped-down holster. Keeps asking for you." Linstrom paused to wipe his hands on a cloth.

Kansas spoke low in his always-deep voice. "He say why?"

"No, but he had a copy of that last dime novel with your face on it. The one that says you're the fastest draw west of the Mississippi."

Kansas knew about the novels and could only guess that a nosy writer he had once encountered up north and turned away had only wanted to get a good look at his face for a later sketch. That image continued to haunt his trail.

In the back of the store, the women looking at ribbons tried to signal Linstrom, but he pretended not to notice. He followed Kansas to the open doorway where they looked up and down the quiet street. No one was stirring in the sunlight. The old man on the bench to their right was snoring softly.

Linstrom gestured across the street at the single saloon. "The kid's still over there, gambling."

"He give a name?"

"No, just Billy. But he tracked you here because that latest dime novel says how you're doing business with the sheriff in this town, bringing in some pretty bad fellows."

"Not anymore. I'm leaving."

"Which direction?"

Kansas shrugged. "I'll decide when I hit the saddle."

"Where is the sheriff?" Linstrom asked.

"Out at some ranch trying to settle things over water rights."

"What'll I tell the kid?"

"Nothing." Kansas showed disinterest because this was not the first time he had run into a young upstart after dime novels started following him. *Lord, don't let this get out of hand.*

He walked on the creaky sidewalk and over to his big roan at the rail. It wore a hackamore instead of a bridle, and it nuzzled Kansas, as he reached into the sack and gave it a lump of sugar. He put the sack and shells into his saddlebag. He lifted the stirrup, tightened the cinch, dropped the stirrup, and stroked the animal's neck. He checked his bedroll and possible sack, all tied down behind his saddle. The canteen on his cantle was full.

Loud voices suddenly rang from the saloon across the street.

Linstrom came out of the store, over to the boardwalk near Kansas, talking low. "There he is now."

Kansas watched as the youth called Billy, wearing shabby clothes, black sack coat, floppy brimmed brown hat, and an old, stiff, leather holster tied down, came out on the boardwalk. He had icy blue eyes, unkempt brown hair, and a cocky demeanor.

Seeing Kansas across the street at his roan, Billy came down from the boardwalk and was about to cross over. Behind Billy, just out the swinging doors, was a cardsharp called Casey—a

3

man in his forties, wearing a fine suit of clothes with a blue-striped vest but without his jacket. Casey wore a gunbelt with silver inlay and a pearl-handled Colt at his right hip.

Coming out of the saloon behind Casey, Bo Chapman—thirties, mean-looking, with dirty red hair, and twin holsters—moved out of the line of fire, but ready to back him up.

Linstrom muttered to Kansas. "Both them fellas drifted in while you were out of town. That's Casey in front. Bo Chapman's the dirty one hanging back."

Linstrom went back into his store, facing the worried women and gesturing them to the back where they would be safe. Linstrom soon returned to his doorway with a Winchester repeater and worked a shell into the chamber.

In front of the saloon, Casey moved north along the warped boardwalk like the sword of death. He stopped at the edge to call out the young gunman, who had stepped out into the dusty street, headed toward Kansas.

"Hey, kid!"

Billy turned slowly, hand on his holster. They faced each other, some twenty feet apart, as Casey's boots hit the dirt.

Two other men coming out of the saloon stopped, and then quickly scrambled back inside.

Billy showed defiance, no fear. His hat shaded his eyes.

Casey berated him. "You palmed that queen."

Billy had his chin out. "You're lying."

"All you got to do is own up," Casey lied, looking for an excuse to gun him down.

Across the street and over by his roan, Kansas watched in silence—he had seen this too many times before. Except this kid looked like he'd never been to town. Kansas felt a fatherly urge to stop it, but he had to wait for his chance. He moved over to his right, out of the line of fire, as did Linstrom.

4

Billy stood transfixed as Casey took a stance.

Bo Chapman stood aside, against the saloon wall, hand on his holster.

Curious men came out along the street from both directions, then hurried to find safety in doorways or back inside, behind windows so they could still watch.

A passing rider turned his horse from the line of fire and retreated.

The old man on the bench near the general store remained asleep, head down.

Billy stood firm, looking like a kid who thought he could take on the world with bravado, when he should really still be in Bible Class, or out cleaning stalls, or hauling wood in for his mother cooking his supper.

Casey smiled like the kiss of death. He worked his fingers by his holster. His lips curved into a sneer. "Come on, kid. Own up."

Billy did not respond, only stood ready.

Casey grew impatient. "I'm through talking. Draw, or I will."

A long moment of silence…

And then Billy went for his sidearm. Casey drew faster and fired. Billy's left arm was hit. With his right, slowly now, Billy managed to drag his weapon from its holster, but he staggered and dropped to one knee on the hard ground. In great pain from the bullet wound to his left arm, Billy raised his weapon in his shaky right hand.

Casey, toying with Billy, fired again. The shot burned Billy's right hand and hit the revolver, sending the Colt to the ground even as the bullet ricocheted across Billy's right side.

Billy grabbed his burned right hand with his left, then his side where blood appeared above his belt. He knelt to gather up his weapon with his left hand. Staggering to his feet and fighting to hold the revolver in both hands, he lifted it to aim at Casey. The weapon swayed.

Casey, tired of the game, aimed now with the deliberate plan to kill. He took his time, aware that the whole town was watching. He was so intent, he didn't see Kansas crossing the street to his left.

Kansas now appeared in Casey's line of sight and moved in front of the helpless youth, who had dropped to his knees. Kansas stood quiet, watching Casey.

"Who the devil are you?" Casey demanded.

In his deep voice, Kansas answered. "I came to smite the wicked."

"Get out of the way."

Chapman stood off to the side, back from Casey, ready to back him up.

"All right, mister. You got a real urge to die," Casey snapped.

"Confess your sins before it's too late," Kansas warned.

Casey snickered, wondering who this weird man in black might be.

At that moment the bartender, parting the swinging doors for a look, called out in a hushed voice. "Casey, let it go. That's Kansas Red." Then he quickly disappeared back inside.

Chapman caught his breath. Casey was stunned. Both had heard tales of Kansas Red's deadly fast draw and bounty hunting success.

The whole town watched from windows and doorways.

Casey swallowed hard, moistened his lips. Wiped his gun hand on his shirt. Taking down Kansas Red would make him famous. He knew that Chapman was thinking the same thing. The two of them could make it happen. If they had the guts.

Kansas stood ready. Hand by his holster.

Casey drew fast. Chapman drew as swift.

But Kansas's Colt was faster, hammer fanned, firing rapidly, before they could even pull the trigger.

Kansas's shots hit Casey in the chest and Chapman's left shoulder.

Chapman's bullet creased Kansas's head above his left ear.

Kansas, stunned, staggered back as he fanned the hammer again. His next shot hit Chapman's forehead, dead center. Chapman slammed back against the wall of the saloon, then slid down on his rump, a dead man staring with glassy eyes.

Casey dropped to his knees and grabbed at his bleeding chest with his right hand. He held his six-gun in his left and aimed it crazily at Kansas, who was still on his feet but staggering.

Kansas, six-gun in hand, vision temporarily blurred, squinted hard, slowly bringing everything into near-focus.

Casey fired. His bullet slammed high into Kansas's right shoulder, his gun arm, spiraling pain down to his elbow. Kansas stumbled for a few feet as his vision cleared, even as he fired back. Blood spread under his shirt and down his sleeve.

Casey, hit twice in the chest, fell onto his back with a thud. Sprawled out, he pulled the trigger again, even as he died. The stray bullet hit the post in front of the saloon. Casey and Chapman, both dead, had lost the gamble.

Kansas, bleeding above his left ear and deep in his right shoulder, was still on his feet, shaking his head.

Billy, stunned and bleeding from his painful left arm, burning right side and traumatized right hand, still knelt on the hard ground. Two merchants came to his aid and got him to his feet.

"Doctor's that way," one said as they half carried him south on the boardwalk. On the bench by the general store, the old man still slept soundly.

Red Linstrom set his rifle aside, hurried out of his store and over to Kansas. He grabbed Kansas by the left arm to steady him.

Kansas, head throbbing, grumbled. "What were you waiting for?"

"Didn't want to spoil your fun. Besides, you were too fast for me to do anything."

They watched as Billy, barely conscious, was carried up the street by two men hurrying him along.

"On his way to the doctor," Linstrom said. "And so are you."

"Take care of my horse," Kansas said, fading.

Kansas wavered even as Linstrom fought to hold him upright. Two ranchers came to help, one on either side of Kansas.

"Listen, Kansas," Linstrom said. "You've got to know. I heard tell that Chapman has a brother, a lot meaner than him and on the dodge, but he'll show, sooner or later. So, watch your back."

Kansas shrugged and thought, *So what else is new?*

Later that afternoon in one of the back rooms of the doctor's office, Kansas lay on his back on a high table and was slowly regaining consciousness. His head above his left ear was bandaged, as was his right shoulder, which felt numb. His head still ached from the crease. He lay quiet but annoyed that his gunbelt and weapon were on a nearby wall hook, out of reach.

Dr. Tillman, in his late sixties, was husky and good-looking with a slight, white beard. It was well known that he would rather be hunting and fishing than cooped up indoors, but he was the only doctor within a hundred miles and finding it hard to retire. His white coat was freshly laundered, but now had sleeves that were soiled red.

"Bullet went right through your shoulder. Missed the bone," Tillman said.

"My horse?"

"In the livery."

"How's the kid?" Kansas murmured.

"In the next room, still sedated. You saved his life. And both hardcases are dead. But don't worry. I'll make it right with the sheriff when he gets back."

Kansas put his hand to his brow in a daze. "What'd you give me?"

"Just something to make you stop fighting me."

Kansas closed his eyes, mumbling to himself but easily heard until he finally slept.

In a dreamworld for hours, Kansas saw images. He was unaware that as he spoke now and then, the doctor questioned him and sometimes got a meaningless answer.

In a haze, Kansas saw himself when he was barely nineteen, standing hidden in trees with his horse and pack mule. Staring across the town square at a church where a colorful wedding was taking place. The bride was blonde and very beautiful.

Then that image faded, and he saw and felt the lonely nights on the prairie and on mountain trails.

Next, he was in a battlefield shrouded in gun smoke, dodging rifle fire and rolling cannon balls while his own rifle became almost too hot to hold. Trying to help other Union soldiers who were wounded, then doing the same for wounded Confederate prisoners. Saying prayers with them. And fighting for his own survival under constant attack.

He saw himself after the war, dressed in black to suit how he felt about his life. Practicing his fast draw until his arm ached. Hauling in an escaped prisoner who had left a battered woman in his wake. Sometimes wearing a badge. But all the time without direction. A lost soul. Just one day at a time, year after year.

He drifted from images to darkness and deep sleep.

Hours later that night in the same back room, Kansas, still dazed and agitated, awakened with the doctor seated at his side.

Kansas slowly got a grasp on where he was. He stared at the ceiling as his mind began to clear.

"What'd you hit me with?" Kansas muttered.

"I had to put you out again." Tillman said as he leaned back in his chair. "By the way, who's Carol?"

Kansas winced, tightened his lips, and looked away to stare at the wall.

Seeing it was a sore subject, Tillman dropped it. "You went on about the war. I know how that was. I went in as an army surgeon."

Kansas murmured something unintelligible. His eyes closed as he went to sleep again.

Dr. Tillman sat back, studying this man and not fully understanding, yet having even more respect for him now that he saw how the man's torment did not stop him from being honorable, law-abiding, and decent. In all of Kansas's nightmare utterings, nothing said any different.

Much later in the night, the doctor had finished removing soiled bandages by lamplight as Kansas awakened, not wearing a shirt. Tillman helped him sit up, steadied him as he swayed, and began applying medication and clean wraps to his shoulder and around his head.

The doctor paused to stare again at Kansas's marked chest and shoulders.

"You got enough scars on you for ten men." He finished the new bandages. "Sheriff came by. I told him how it all happened. You and the boy are in the clear."

Dazed and woozy, Kansas lay back down, closing his eyes again.

*   *

At first light, Kansas woke with a clear head and vision. Sunlight glistened on the one window in the back room. He allowed the doctor to sit him up and help him get his shirt on. His boots felt cold. His hat rested on his sticky, dark hair, his right arm in a sling. He felt pain in that shoulder. He worked his right hand and fingers—they were good and limber, at least.

He managed to follow Tillman into the front office, then sat down, exhausted.

Tillman gave him coffee, bread, and a slice of roast beef. Kansas ate hungrily and asked for more coffee.

"You got no business riding out so soon," Tillman said. "On the other hand, the sheriff worries that Chapman's brother will show up before you're out of here. Seems that after the fight, some friend of Chapman's took off in a hurry."

"And the kid?"

"Outside, somewhere. Been a real nuisance." The doctor cleaned his instruments in a tray by a side window, which was dirty on the outside, blurring the sunlight, and which reflected his image. Next to the tray, a wooden mallet and stacks of books beside a half-empty cup of cold coffee.

Tillman checked Kansas's eyes. "That crease above your ear barely missed doing you in. I saw a lot of it in the war, but you have a really hard head. Any problem with your vision? Headache?"

Kansas shook his head. He did have a headache but wanted out of there.

The front door opened as Billy Cassidy came inside, closing it behind him. The youth's left arm was in a sling and his right hand was lightly bandaged. He still wore the old sidearm, looking bright-eyed and bushy-tailed, ready for more trouble.

Billy spoke directly to Kansas. "I've been waiting for you. I got your roan all saddled and packed. I told 'em I was your son."

11

"Young man, you take it easy," Tillman said.

"I need you to go with me," Billy fussed at Kansas. "It's a matter of life or death."

The doctor looked as if he'd heard that a dozen times.

"We got to get south to Walsenburg," Billy urged. "And then west."

"Walsenburg," Tillman remarked. "That's where they're digging coal."

"My pa will pay anything you ask," the boy added.

Kansas, acting disinterested, got to his feet, wavering a bit. He reached for his gunbelt on the nearby wall hook and strapped it on. He checked the load in his weapon, finding the doctor had reloaded it for him, and he slid it back into the holster.

"Thanks," he said to Tillman. He fumbled in his vest pocket, then gave a silver dollar to the doctor. They shook hands.

"I hope you have a clean shirt in your pack," the doctor said.

Kansas nodded. Unsteady, he walked out the front door, blinded by the early sun until he tugged down on his hat brim. Billy was on his heels, following him to the hitching rail where both horses stood saddled and loaded with gear. Next to Kansas's big blue roan, Billy's aging sorrel stood half asleep.

Up and down the street, no one was in sight.

Kansas lifted the stirrup, checked on the tightness of the cinch. Satisfied, he dropped the stirrup as his roan turned to nuzzle him. He was a bit surprised it had allowed someone else to saddle him.

Billy checked his own cinch. He was bursting with impatience.

Kansas paused, looked the youth up and down. What he saw was a mess. Yet he had enough curiosity to see what the kid was fussing about. Besides, he saw himself in the boy at that same age, a cocky youth ready to take on the whole world.

Billy reached inside his coat, pulled out a damp and battered dime novel with Kansas's image drawn on the cover, offered it.

Kansas, recognizing it, ignored him, mounted and reined about. Billy had not challenged him to a fight, so his claim of 'life or death' just might be real. Kansas was in no hurry to hear more of it, but strangely enough, he headed south toward the rolling hills and open, golden grassland.

Billy shoved the novel inside his coat, quickly mounted, and followed at a safe distance.

Back in the doctor's front office, Tillman yawned as he returned to cleaning his instruments. He set aside the wooden mallet which had bopped many a knee. He sipped the cold coffee, made a face and yawned again. He had plans to sleep the rest of the day.

Then the front door swung open. It was seventy-year-old Dan Tucker, a cranky retired gunsmith with a very patient wife. Tucker was hatless with shaggy, grey hair, a trimmed beard, and a distinctive bump on his nose, and he wore a soiled, light blue shirt over his britches. Tillman could see a story coming, again, and fought to keep a straight face.

Tucker had blood and a big knot on the left side of his head, near the crown. He staggered to a chair and sat down. He looked self-satisfied with a silly grin. None of this was new to Tillman.

"Okay, Dan, what happened this time?"

"Doc, it's my wife. She swung at me, so I ducked and fell out of my chair and hit my head on the stove."

"Why did she do that?"

Tucker had to chuckle. "Oh, just because I patted her on the rump and said how fat she was. That's all."

"And?"

Tillman was checking the wound, the lump, Tucker's eyes and ears.

Tucker giggled. "I mighta said she waddled like an old sow."

The doctor hid his grin as he treated the head wound. "So maybe you had had a few drinks?"

"Yeah, but I was only having fun with her." Tucker made a face at his discomfort. "Is my head cracked, Doc?"

"No, but can you see okay?"

"Yeah. Just hungry. She didn't feed me."

Tillman bandaged Tucker's head as much as was possible.

All of a sudden, the front door swung open and slammed shut behind a very large man.

Slim Chapman, a mean-eyed, red-bearded grizzly of a man— and brother to the man Kansas had shot the day before— charged in like a bull. Dirty red hair to his shoulders and a crooked mustache, in his fifties, with a big belly hanging over his belt, he wore a well-oiled sidearm in a tied-down holster on his right hip. Chapman stopped when he saw Dan Tucker being treated in the doctor's chair.

Tillman hardly looked at him but had a good view of him in the window reflection. "Have a seat. I'll be with you in a moment."

Slim sat on the edge of a chair, making vile faces.

Tillman dragged out the treatment, then stood back as Dan got to his feet. "From now on, stick to whispering sweet nothings to your wife."

"Yeah, Doc, sure. If she don't lock me out of the house."

At that moment, Mrs. Tucker—a pretty greying woman in her late sixties, wearing a white apron over her blue gingham dress, and being only a bit chubby—charged inside. She ignored Slim and walked straight over to her sheepish husband.

Tillman tried not to smile. "He's fine, Mrs. Tucker. But if he has vision problems or trouble with his balance, bring him back."

Tucker let her help him to his feet. "Doc, what do we owe you?"

"A dollar," Tillman said with a flickering smile.

Mrs. Tucker reached in her apron pocket for some coins and counted them out in the palm of the doctor's hand. Then she put her arm around her husband and lovingly marched him outside. Tillman watched them leave with a grin.

At the same time, Tillman knew his other visitor was big trouble. Slim looked enough like his brother Bo to cause alarm. Casually, his back to the man, Tillman continued to clean his instruments but slid the tray closer to the wooden mallet. He watched Slim's reflection in the window.

Slim waited until Dan and his wife are out the door, closing it behind them. Now he charged to his feet, fierce and threatening even while being ignored.

"Where is he?" Slim snarled, angry at seeing only Tillman's back.

Tillman appeared disinterested. "What's your problem? If it's a toothache, the only dentist we have is also the barber. Down the street."

"I know he was here," Slim snapped. "He killed my brother."

"Who?"

"Kansas Red!"

Tillman remained casual. "Oh, him. He left hours ago."

"Where'd he go?"

"He didn't say, but you can ask the sheriff. He's back in town."

Reflected in the dirty window for the doctor to see, Slim Chapman drew his six-gun and aimed it at Tillman's back. He stood only a few feet away and lowered his weapon, aiming it at the doctor's rear.

"You'd better tell me or I'll shoot you in the rump."

When Slim pulled back the hammer, finger on the trigger,

Dr. Tillman grabbed the mallet, spun with it in his hand and slammed it into Slim's gun hand, sending the weapon flying. Slim yelped in pain. Tillman swung again and hit him hard in the fat of his belly, below his ribs. The mallet landed hard on his left boot.

Slim gasped, eyes bugged out, and doubled up, breathless, hopping at the pain in his foot, hand, and belly. He grabbed his middle with his left hand and fell to his knees in shock.

Dr. Tillman set aside the mallet and leaned over to retrieve the weapon.

"You ought to see a doctor for your breathing problem."

Slim sneered up at him but was helpless.

"Get up," Tillman said. "The sheriff loves a good story."

At that moment, an echoing shot brought two merchants charging inside, followed by the sheriff, a husky middle-aged man with a Colt revolver in his hand.

"Sheriff," Tillman said, "this gentleman was just coming to see you and give himself up."

CHAPTER TWO

While Slim Chapman was dragged to the sheriff's office and jail that morning, and while Dr. Tillman finally found time to sleep, Billy followed the trail south from town, keeping Kansas in sight not too far ahead of him as they both rode at a walk.

They crossed the silent tracks of the Kansas Pacific and continued south.

Aside from cattle on distant golden hills and an occasional homestead, the land was wide open and mostly barren of trees. Above in the sky, a red-tailed hawk soared on the wind, and more than once, a jack rabbit jumped into their path, startling their mounts.

They came upon a dozen pronghorn antelopes, which leaped from salt brush and sped away like the hopping rabbits, but twice as fast.

The day wore on, and soon came a red sunset beyond a rise of rocky hills off to the west, and the far distant blue shadow of the snow-capped Rockies.

With twilight, long shadows fell on rough country with its blue grama grass, occasional clumps of brush, and imposing rocky hills. The trail swung west to a wide but shallow water hole, rimmed by cottonwoods and fed by a little creek from a spring up in the rocky crest. The ground was marked by many hoof prints, some unshod, and with critter prints as well.

Kansas knew all along he was being followed. He also knew that sooner or later, Billy would get his story out in the open. A loner most of his life, Kansas seldom took to company, but the boy was such a mess, not even wearing his gunbelt in a safe position, Kansas could not stop feeling the need to help him.

Night came and a bright moon guided them.

When Kansas turned off the trail to the creek and waterhole, Billy closed the distance and rode over to him. Kansas reined up, ignoring the youth as he dismounted and rested his roan. He lifted a stirrup and loosened the cinch, then knelt by what had been a campfire near the pond, stirring the ashes with a stick. It was days old.

Billy, exasperated, swung down from the saddle.

"Hey, mister, I don't care sour grapes about you. I'm broke and foot-sore, and you got to listen."

Billy offered the novel again, holding it up in the moonlight. Kansas ignored it and stood up to walk over to the water, his roan following. The water was dirty, as if some traveler had bathed in it, but he let his mount drink from it. He unsaddled and put his gear aside.

Billy led his sorrel to the water and also unsaddled. Impatient in the cold moonlight, he still held the bound paper issue in his hand. It had a good likeness of Kansas on the cover.

Kansas frowned as he sat on a nearby rock. "Build us a fire and get some coffee going. There's beans in my possible."

Billy shoved the novel back inside his shirt. Frustrated, he gathered chips and some chunks of dry brush. He got a fire going as Kansas brought forth his possible sack and started some coffee, using pond water filtered through a cloth.

Billy looked about to explode with his anxiety.

I must be getting soft, Kansas thought of his abiding Billy's persistence. He couldn't explain why he felt connected to the youth.

Kansas set out a pan and cans of beans, dragging things out while they cleaned their tin plates, and then sat back with their really strong coffee in the firelight. He knew the youth was chomping at the bit, but from experience, he also knew it best to slow things down.

A bright moon and stars added a glow to the surrounding terrain. Somewhere in the distance, a coyote howled. Within seconds, it was answered by another further away. They barked and howled until Billy covered his ears.

Finally the night was quiet. Kansas gestured an okay to Billy.

Quickly, the youth, seated close by, leaned forward with the novel in hand. "My pa's ranch is over in Slippery Hills. They call it that 'count of mud slides and flash floods. It's way far west, just at the start of the high country."

Appearing disinterested, Kansas yet was curious about the youth's problem.

Billy, now that he had an audience, was careful to pick his words. "Back in Kansas, Ma had been getting letters from one prison or another. From that outlaw, Thorn Larson. The last one came from Canon City, in Colorado."

Kansas' eyes narrowed, turned icy cold, hard. *Larson.* He downed his coffee though he wanted to spit it out, feeling choked. He knew he was not going to like the rest of the story.

Billy shoved the novel into his belt. "Pa got real mad, burned the letters. Ma said how Larson had bothered her before she got married but she'd been afraid to tell my pa. So Pa found out that Larson had ended up in Canon City prison. For life. But just the same, Pa sold out his freight business and moved us way out here over a year ago. He cut all ties, never told anyone in Kansas where we were going. Ma wasn't happy about being stuck out there on the ranch. We got hardly any neighbors at all."

Kansas remained silent as he tried to handle the youth's story, afraid of what was coming next.

"Pa never stopped worrying about Larson. And then he saw your face on the novel, and it said where you was, so he made me track you down. Pa said you were the only one could maybe stop Larson if he ever showed up."

Kansas sipped his coffee, stared into the night.

Billy drew a deep breath. "And then, a few days after I left the ranch to find you, I heard some fellow saying as how Larson had busted out with his gang and got chased. Posse lost them in a big snow storm in the high Rockies. Found two of 'em frozen and sticking out of an avalanche, so they figured the lot of them had died in it, and nobody wanted to dig them out or end up the same way."

No reaction from Kansas, who had known of the escape and presumed deaths. He had his own score to settle with Larson, which he thought had ended with the same news.

Kansas tried to sip more coffee and could not. He was rocked with turmoil and now feared the youth's answer. "What's your name?"

"Billy. Billy Cassidy."

Kansas slowly and painfully set his cup down by the crackling fire. He stared at the yellow flames. He then got to his feet and turned his back, staring across the water hole at the dark hills. The beat of his heart was painful. He had trauma running down his spine, sweat on his brow.

Kansas's voice dragged. "And your pa's name?"

"Sam Cassidy."

"And your ma?"

"Carol."

Unable to turn to face the boy, Kansas asked, "How old are you?"

Billy, annoyed at the delay, snapped. "Seventeen. Almost."

"You have other kinfolk?"

"No, all gone, both sides. Pa had a kid brother, Jack. Got killed in the War Between the States."

Kansas hesitated. "And at your ranch? Any fire power?"

"Just my pa. Two hands who can't hit the side of a barn. And an old man does some garden stuff. But there's my ma's friend, Leslie Allen, visiting from Texas. She shoots better than I do, but..." Billy became exasperated. "You gonna help us or not?"

Kansas, not recognizing the friend's name, delayed his answer. "You palm that card like they said?"

Startled and even more annoyed, Billy spat it out. "Sure I did, but he was cheating first. I just..."

"Cheated."

"Yeah, but don't tell my pa. He'd have a fit."

Kansas calmly sat back down and poured himself some more coffee. "How far is the ranch?"

"Long way off in the mountains. Maybe a week or more."

"Better get some sleep. I'll take first watch."

"So you're coming?"

"Only way to settle you down."

Suddenly exhausted, Billy went for his bedroll.

Later, while Billy slept, Kansas sat staring at the stars and moon reflected in the dark water hole. Painful memories and a miserable history haunted him into the night.

One thing he knew for sure. If Larson was still alive, he had a lot to answer for, and Kansas yearned to make him pay.

*   *   *   *

The next afternoon, while Billy and Kansas crossed the tracks of the Atchison Topeka & Santa Fe and headed southwest toward Walsenburg, the Cassidy ranch was about to be hit.

A storm was moving into the Slippery Hills from the north with dark clouds. A light drizzle had begun. It was freezing cold.

The ranch headquarters sat isolated from its neighbors by deep, rolling, grassy hills that were sprinkled with yellow wild flowers and lightly wooded with stately dark pines, quivering green aspen, and occasional broadleaf cottonwoods. Corrals and outbuildings were set north and way off from the house on slightly rolling ground. Over in the distant, higher terrain, mixed cattle could be seen grazing. Beyond to the far west rose snow-capped ridges leading to the great Rocky Mountains.

South of and on lower ground than the out buildings, the two-story house with fading white paint had a garden with spring blooms and a white-washed picket fence. In front of the garden gate, a buggy with a black horse stood waiting.

Over at the barn in the mist, two of the ranch hands, Antonio, barely twenty, and Pedro, twice his age, were turning two colts out into the corral. They spoke in Spanish and joked, laughing. Pedro's uncle, the gardener, was in town, escorting the cook.

Coming from the house and uphill toward the barn, rancher Sam Cassidy, forty-five years old with greying hair, limped along with an empty bucket. A handsome man with a strong jaw and clean-shaven, yet he looked tired of a lot more than work.

With Sam was Sly Walker, middle aged and hefty, a visiting neighbor. They wore long coats and had left the women in the house for some fresh air and escape. Only Sly wore a side arm. Sam, a former merchant, seldom wore a gun, especially when out to do a chore.

Neither seemed to care about the light drizzling rain which rested on their hat brims and would soon drip. The sky was ever darkening.

"I can't keep up with our wives," Sly said in a southern accent. He chuckled with a nod back toward the house. "Ribbons, dresses, town gossip. God bless 'em."

"Except for Leslie. She's a real Texan," Sam remarked.

"Yeah," Sly said with a grin. "How'd she end up here?"

"Her ma and Carol's, they were good friends from when they were back East in finishing school," Sam offered. "But when the Allens came up from Texas for our wedding, Leslie was pretty young and more interested in horses than the young fellows hanging around her."

"How can you remember that far back?" Sly grinned at him.

"Hey, you're no spring chicken either."

Sly gestured back to the house. "So with the cook being in town getting supplies, and the housekeeper away, I have to ask, can your wife actually cook?"

"No, but I didn't marry her for that." Sam grinned. "First time I saw her, I was a goner."

"Well, sir, Marianne's baked beans and blueberry pie won me over a week after we met."

They laughed as they neared the barn. Two men with different lives, different women, and yet very good friends.

At the same time, on a far off hill overlooking the ranch, danger lurked.

Hidden by a stand of tall, dark pines, nine mounted men were watching the ranch under a darkening sky and light sprinkle. They had two saddle horses on lead and a pack horse. Their leader was Thorn Larson, a good-looking, clean-shaven man with a rugged scar high on his left cheek. From under his hat, light brown scraggly hair reached down to his shoulders. His bandanna was red-and-white striped.

Larson was astride his pinto gelding.

With him were three members of his original gang, all in their forties. Leech and Rumson were both balding and bearded. Thatch, riding a black gelding with white marks, was the youngest with long, blond hair, mustache, and trimmed beard, a hefty man who looked more like a wrestler. And it was known Thatch could not keep his hands off of any available women.

Joining in the prison escape and still with them were the Longley brothers, Buck and Sid. Both were convicted killers who had no respect for the life of anyone or anything. Larson was only biding his time to be rid of them, knowing it would not be easy.

In addition, Turner and Target, who also broke out with them and came along for the ride, had been convicted rustlers. They both had bellies hanging over their belts. They were the jolly pair who took nothing seriously. Turner did entertain them all with his mouth harp on occasion. Larson didn't think much of them, but he kept them along as throw-aways.

Also with the gang was Charlie, a solemn, inscrutable Ute in his fifties, wearing ranch clothes and a hat with a woven red band. He was hired in prison as a tracker who kept his distance from the others, not because he feared them as they liked to believe, but because he looked down on them as less than animals. Yes, Charlie had been up for horse stealing, but he had figured it was his right. Now he expected to be paid for keeping these bad ones alive in the mountains and getting them to their hideout to the west.

Down below and inside the luxuriously furnished parlor of the ranchhouse, Sam's wife, Carol Cassidy, just turned thirty-six, was overly pretty with golden brown hair to her shoulders and held back from her face by jeweled combs. Wearing a blue satin dress the color of her eyes, she played a few notes on the recently tuned rosewood piano. Weak light came through lace at the front windows.

There was a dwindling fire in the hearth, which was set further back. A collection of framed tintypes and photographic images lined the mantle.

Carol returned to an ornate chair near the coffee table where she had set a silver tea service on a tray, across from the sofa.

With a full-time cook and housekeeper, Carol never had to get her hands dirty. Not since the day she had married Sam. Even now, she would stop to admire the diamonds on her left hand. Yes, she had married well.

Today, with the cook in town and the housekeeper having a day off with her own family, Carol had forced herself to make the tea. She sat forward to be sure it had brewed, then served it.

On the sofa across from her sat Marianne Walker, a comely brunette in her mid-forties, lovely in a blue gingham dress with a gold cross dangling from a necklace. A sweet woman with ranch upbringing, she had managed a happy life with her husband who was always hungry and a little wild. With few neighbors, Marianne had learned to accept Carol's vanity, seeing it as more of a problem for Carol herself. She often read inner turmoil in Carol's practiced ways and felt sorry for her.

They sipped tea and chatted.

"I didn't see your son when we arrived," Marianne said with a New England accent.

"Sam sent him on an errand a week ago. That's all I know," Carol said truthfully, then paused with amusement. "I think Billy just wears him out. Young people have so much energy."

"I thought maybe he was off to school."

25

"Sam taught him his letters and wanted him to go to mining school, but Billy would rather just work on the ranch. The two of them are always hunting and fishing, or going to horse auctions. He just wants to be with his father."

"And his mother?" Marianne asked, smiling.

"I'm just decoration," Carol said.

Carol had no idea of Billy's real mission. She only knew that whatever it was, it had calmed Sam down from some unspoken inner stress.

Marianne, always smiling, didn't let on that she had figured out from the wedding date that Billy was born two months early. It did please her to feel that Carol was not so perfect after all.

"Decoration," Marianne repeated with some envy. "But your friend Leslie said at your wedding, she could see all the young men were in love with you."

Carol smiled, accepting the story because it pleased her. "When I married Sam, the Allens came up from Texas for the wedding. That's when I first met Leslie. She was a bridesmaid and barely sixteen, and I know full well that she was wearing her boots under her skirts."

Marianne laughed. "She's such a Texan."

Carol smiled. "And you are a Bostonian married to a southerner. How did that happen?"

Marianne flushed. "I met Sly on a trip to New Orleans, at a New Year's Eve dance. My father disowned me when I married him. But strangely enough, Sly's family accepted me and set about turning me into a Southern belle. They could see how much we loved each other."

"But you were from Massachusetts, and he fought for the south."

"I loved him, no matter what." Marianne paused, smiled. "Just as you get along fine with Leslie."

"We both lost our parents a few years ago, so I imagine she's lonely, and having her visit breaks the monotony." Carol sipped her tea and suddenly laughed. "I have to tell you, at our wedding reception, I could also see that Leslie was smitten with Sam, but she was so young, I kind of laughed it off."

"Oh, my."

Carol paused to reflect. "She might have been a good choice for Sam's kid brother, Jack, who had been back East studying for the ministry, but he wasn't at the wedding, and then he joined the army, so they never met."

"From the ministry to being a soldier?"

"Yes, it was strange," Carol said. "And sad to say, Jack died in the war."

Carol remembered how she had liked young Jack but that he had been too poor for her needs. She had had many beaus before marrying the wealthy Sam. Seemingly satisfied with her choice, she poured a little more tea as Marianne persisted.

"Did Sam join the army?" Marianne asked, curious.

"No, he was too busy keeping his freight shipments going to help the North."

Carol paused to pour more of the hot tea.

Marianne hesitated. "Do you think Leslie never married because of Sam?"

"Oh no, she got over that in a hurry, like young girls do. In fact she's been betrothed two times. The first died in the last year of the war, fighting for the South. The other died when a bronc fell on him about a year ago."

"That's so sad," Marianne responded. "But I think she needs someone just as tough as she is, I mean, to make her happy."

Carol laughed. "I don't think anyone is as tough as she is."

Marianne nodded but actually envied Leslie's spirit.

Carol envied no one she knew. She enjoyed being so refined

and beautiful in contrast to Leslie's rough Texas ways. She secretly took pleasure in Sam choosing her and never having shown any interest in the socially inept Texan. She also tolerated Marianne being such a homemaker because there were so few women in the area. Carol enjoyed the differences, always placing herself above others, because without the ability to rise above others, she would have felt like she was nothing.

Carol ignored Marianne's often unspoken questions, such as, if Sam was so rich back in Kansas, why did he move out to the middle of nowhere?

Yes, Carol knew the answer and would never speak of it. She also knew that sometimes what you wanted most could be the very thing one would never have.

A short time later, Leslie Allen—a strikingly beautiful outdoor woman just turned thirty-four—entered the house from the back. She had very long, light golden hair flowing in waves down to her waist, large crystal-blue eyes, and an uncommon grace. She always seemed to be harboring secrets, thoughts, and unspoken opinions, which sometimes aggravated Carol. She wore a long, blue riding skirt that just covered her boot tops, and a white blouse under her blue jacket. On her right wrist was a wide, gold bracelet with turquoise stones, which had been her mother's, and which she treasured dearly.

Leslie stopped to stoke up the fire and added another chunk of wood.

"Raining," Leslie said, removing her wide brimmed hat. "I saw lightning in the hills. Going to be one heck of a storm."

Now they could hear the wind as it hit the windows and roof. Sudden hail drummed on and battered the house. It sounded like gunfire when it hit.

"Oh, dear," Marianne said. "I hope we can get home okay."

"You could stay over," Carol said.

Leslie slumped down on the couch next to Marianne.

Carol smiled sweetly at Leslie. "My dear, you treat that rifle like the only love in your life. How do you expect to find a husband if you out-shoot and out-ride them?"

Leslie didn't express her thoughts aloud, but in her heart she knew, *You can trust a rifle, but I'm not so sure about the rest.*

"Leave her be," Marianne admonished. "I'm glad to see someone meet men on their own terms. But, Leslie, where is your rifle?"

"On the back porch," Leslie said. "I have to clean it before I bring it in here."

Carol daintily sipped her tea. "Yes, that's a house rule. I dislike the smell of gun oil."

"It would take away the nice scent of the rosewood," Marianne said to Carol with a smile. "I do envy you for marrying so well. As for me, we just make ends meet. I saved my egg money for two years, and all I wanted was a new dress and a coat. He used it to buy a cow dog instead."

"But," Leslie said to Marianne, "you would not trade your husband for anyone."

Marianne laughed softly. "You are so right."

Carol had a strange look on her face. Having nice things made up for the dust and hardships. She knew how to make Sam happy, and he treated her like a queen, always catering to her every whim. Yet, it was lonely for her with no society to impress.

Leslie knew Carol's need for comfort and attention, but being here reminded her of life when she still had her mother. *I know, Mom,* she thought, *I belong in Texas, but you're not there. And Carol's okay as she is because she can't help it. She thinks without her finery and riches, she would be nothing at all. But Marianne has an open heart and so easy to be with.'*

"Leslie," Marianne said, "I hope you're staying for the spring dance in town. I know it's a long way to travel, but…"

"She is," Carol mused. "We already have rooms reserved at the hotel. And I have three perfect men lined up for her. The banker's son. The new dentist. And the new doctor."

Leslie pretended disdain, then laughed.

"So, free loans and free doctoring," Marianne offered.

"I'd rather visit the hot springs," Leslie said, "but Carol is so thoughtful, and I don't mind. I'll just keep riding through the herd until I find that one he-bull that's worthy of a Texan."

Marianne laughed while Carol just smiled, always keeping herself above the others by her manner and with her husband's wealth.

Leslie sipped her tea, lifting her little finger as if mocking Carol.

"And," Leslie added, "it's a little late, but I still plan to have six children."

"Trust me," Marianne said, "it's no picnic. Both our daughters went East to school and got married back there. We get letters, but that's all."

There was a moment of silence as the women reflected on their own lives.

No one asked Carol why she had stopped after having Billy. They could only imagine that maybe she was preserving her figure or trying to maintain her youth.

Because of the storm with its hail pounding the roof and the roaring wind, the women could not hear the explosive gunfire out at the barn as the outlaws closed in for the kill and left no one alive, including Sam Cassidy.

Inside the house, the women paused to listen to the loud deluge that shook the house itself. They fell silent and sipped their tea.

Now a log in the fire crashed onto the coals. Leslie got up and went to stoke the fire and move the log back from the front grill. She stood a long time staring at the hot embers.

Why am I so alone? she thought. *Two men wanted to marry me and I wasn't sure, and then I lost them both. Am I just bad luck? Lord, is there anyone out there who will be with me and love me and fight for me? Someone to share my life? Someone I can respect?*

Discouraged, she turned to look back at the happily married Marianne, who she envied, and the socially ambitious Carol, who reigned in the middle of nowhere.

Leslie shrugged to herself. *Who am I to judge?*

Returning to her friends, Leslie sat close to the tea service.

"Our men must be riding it out in the barn," Marianne said.

They tried to make small talk but the storm was so loud, they fell silent again.

Finally, Carol spoke up. "I worry about the house roof. Last time, the barn lost half of its cover."

"At least we don't have twisters here," Marianne said, remembering southern storms and terrifying tornadoes. "You wouldn't have a house by now."

"In Texas," Leslie said, "if a twister shows up, we just rope and tie it down."

Marianne laughed but the loud hail was making Carol too nervous to think anything humorous.

Then suddenly, the front door burst open with a rush of wind, rain and hail, along with two terrifying men in slickers with pistols drawn.

CHAPTER THREE

While rain and hail pounded the Cassidy ranchhouse, Buck Longley and Thatch, two vicious men in slickers, broke into the house and charged the parlor with pistols drawn. They smelled of sweat, rain, and leather.

Leslie grabbed the heavy silver teapot and threw it at Thatch. He knocked it aside as she rushed him, trying to grab his pistol. He slammed his fist into her jaw, knocking her unconscious on her feet. He caught her up and threw her over his shoulder, holding her with more than a little interest, as Thatch had a craze for feisty women.

Marianne screamed her husband's name as Buck grabbed her by the throat. "No use, lady, they're all dead."

Choked until unconscious by Buck, Marianne was lifeless as he lifted her over his shoulder like a sack of wheat.

Carol sat wide-eyed and numb in her chair as Thorn Larson came inside with a slicker in hand. He hesitated only a moment as he drank in her loveliness. In shock, Carol did not speak or resist as Larson walked over, wrapped the slicker around her, picked her up in his arms, swung her around, and headed outside.

Their departure left the door swinging wildly in the wind with hail beating across the plush carpet.

Later that day, the cook would return from town in the wagon, driven by an elderly ranch hand, as hail beat on them, and they discovered the loss of life.

*   *   *   *

Four days after the raid, the hail storm ended. It continued to be cloudy but with only an occasional sprinkle. The outlaws gathered in a sheltered camp in rocky, wooded terrain. It had been a hectic ride to escape detection and disappear into the high reaches of the rugged foothills. Now they felt safe.

They set up tarps in the pines and aspens. They ate and had coffee with a good-sized cookfire, but with nightfall and no rain, that fire was allowed to go out to avoid discovery, as it might be seen a great distance away in the night. They huddled in blankets near smaller pit fires.

Carol, tears on her face, sat by herself near a separate pit fire which was dwindling, and was miserable about her satin dress being ruined.

She was unable to see through the trees to where Leslie and Marianne were sitting with blankets around them and their backs resting on rocks under the aspens, while under constant watch from across the small clearing. They had finished a dish of beans and now savored hot coffee. Come sack time, they were told they would have their hands rebound in front of them.

Marianne, who had been soaked in the storm on leaving the ranch, was ailing from the wet and cold. She was also tearful and painfully upset about losing her husband, and was so in fear for her own life, she had no hope beyond relying on her friendship with Carol. Yet, she couldn't help but notice that there was something odd about Carol's demeanor, as if she already knew Thorn Larson.

Marianne also noticed how Larson was protecting Carol and keeping her to himself.

She was too far away to hear Carol whisper to Larson, as she noted his striped bandanna. "You still have my scarf."

He stroked the bandanna. "I'm never without it."

Carol almost made a joke about it maybe needing to be washed, but caught herself.

Meanwhile, far out of earshot and unable to see Carol's interaction with Larson, Leslie was trying to plan an escape in order to bring help, knowing that the now-sickly Marianne wouldn't last a day on the run. She was also aware that Thatch kept watching her with evil intent. That could work to her advantage. She could see the horses down in the trees, under guard, and was gauging her chances should the opportunity arise.

Above on a ledge looking down on the camp under moving clouds in the cold night, Thorn Larson stood with stolen army field glasses. Wearing a heavy coat, he looked back down along the rough trails. Then he scanned the snowy high ridges north of the red canyons, and down over the green, grassy hills. He lowered the glasses as Thatch climbed up to him and reported.

"Rumson's still bleeding."

Rumson, an original member of Larson's gang, had some importance, but could easily be discarded if Larson so chose.

Larson again scanned the back trails.

"What about a posse?" Thatch asked.

"No chance of one in all that rain and hail. Not even Charlie could have tracked us after that. And even now, with the storm gone, I figure they'll be at least two or three days behind us, if they even figure out which direction we headed." Larson said.

"But we gotta move fast, just in case. Charlie's up ahead now, scouting a way through the cliffs."

"I can't stand that Indian."

Larson was ever amused by the way Charlie got Thatch so riled. "Hey, he hasn't let us down yet. He got us out of that avalanche in the nick of time, or we'd still be up there, buried under a mountain of snow."

"I don't know. He never talks. Just makes out like he's better'n us. And he sneaks around." Thatch pushed his hat back. "Comes the time we don't need him, I want the pleasure. He'll go down real easy."

"I wouldn't bet on that," Larson said, amused.

"Why wait?"

"He knows the mountains. Without him, we could end up lost and dead." Larson said. "Besides, he keeps his mouth shut."

Thatch didn't get it. He also didn't know Larson's plans, except they were headed for a hideout only known to Larson, with the promise of a big share of gold.

Silent awhile, Larson let his thoughts wander down to where Carol huddled alone by a fire. She was worth every second of every day of his life, with so many years to catch up on and every minute with her to savor. Larson had only loved one woman in his life, and now he had her back, for good.

Thatch suddenly gestured toward the camp below. "The men are already fighting among themselves, over the women."

"They better settle down."

Thatch grinned. "I like the young Texan. She's gonna put up a heck of a fight."

Larson looked at Thatch's snear, didn't like what he saw. "My lady hears or sees one bad act, you're dead."

Thatch got the message and would plan accordingly, but he wasn't deterred. "Yeah, so what about Rumson?"

Larson lowered his field glasses and walked down the steep incline with Thatch on his heels. They bypassed the camp and entered a small isolated clearing where Rumson lay covered in blankets with no one tending him. His gear was nearby.

A bloody Rumson, trying to talk, stared up at them.

Thatch shook his head. "He's gonna really slow us down."

"Sorry, old friend," Larson said to the wounded man. He pulled his revolver, stopped, holstered it. He then pulled his hunting knife.

Rumson's eyes grew round with horror.

After the large cook fire was out and having had a little too much whiskey, the outlaws shared small pit fires as they settled down for the night, taking turns on guard. Only an occasional drizzle remained as the sky slowly cleared to uncover the stars and rising moon.

The damp pines lay a heavy scent on the night.

Now and then, an unseen critter stirred in the bushes and up in the rocks.

Wrapped in blankets, sitting against rocks under the aspens and off by themselves, Leslie pretended to sleep as Marianne finally closed her eyes.

Carol and Larson had their own camp, hidden away from the rest and out of earshot. Leslie had been able to see Carol until Larson hung a tarp from trees that covered where they rested. He further repositioned it so that it obstructed any view of them and their pit fire.

Blankets around her, Carol did not object as Larson put his arm around her and took her hand in his. She had just removed her wedding ring, having let it disappear in the grass, and welcomed his affection, but fussed over her attire.

"Thorn, my dress is ruined," she complained.

"Don't worry. You'll have a house full." He kissed her fingers.

Carol shivered as she leaned close to him. "I was afraid you wouldn't find me, way out here."

"I got your last letter in Canon City, just before I broke out."

"I had to bribe the cook to mail it." She wiped at her eyes. "I didn't know if you even received it. But when the newspaper said you had died in the snow, I cried all night."

She didn't say that Sam had been so worried about her tears, he had stayed awake the whole night to hold her. She pushed the thought from her mind. No matter how good Sam had been to her, she had only ever loved one man, and that was Larson.

Larson reflected on the escape. "We did lose two men in a monstrous avalanche. The posse must have figured we were all under it and didn't bother to dig. But we have the Indian with us, a Ute. He saved our hides from getting snowed under. And he knows mountains, but we had to take our time getting here, making sure no one was after us."

Carol loved the comfort of his hand, his presence, but she was worried.

"What about my friends?" she asked, knowing they were prisoners out in the dark.

"I told you, honey, we'll let 'em go just as soon as we can. We couldn't leave witnesses at the ranch to tell the law who we are and how we're still alive. And for now, you wouldn't want me to turn your friends loose in this forsaken country. I'm not a bad man, Carol."

He squeezed her hand, and she responded with the same.

"But why did Sam have to die?" she asked, suddenly tearful.

"That wasn't planned," Larson lied. "He had a rifle in the barn, put up a fight."

"Were you the one who...?"

"No, one of the men." Lying again, he had no intention of

telling her he had made it his personal task to gun down the unarmed Sam in the muddy corral. He could never abide Sam's being alive, not when Sam and Carol had shared more than a handshake for so many years. It had been imperative that Sam no longer exist.

Yet Carol would not easily forget the man she had married. A tear rolled down her cheek.

"Carol, honey, at least you're free, and I have a lot of money stashed. A lot of gold coin. What's more, I was brought up to be a gentleman. And I know what fork to use. You'll have a mansion, French gowns, servants. And you'll be celebrated."

"But how…?"

"I got friends in California, where we can set sail. We'll change our names and we'll soon be living high off the hog. Maybe some big city down in South America."

She leaned toward him with affection. "Your men might give us away."

"They'll be well taken care of. More than any reward. But first, we have to get to the hideout. My cousins are meeting us there with everything we need to get away."

"Is it really possible?"

"The way we always dreamed," he said, suddenly restless. "But I got to ask, where is the kid?"

"Billy's away on a trip, but Sam was his idol. He'll never come with us."

Larson felt nothing for Billy but was interested—until she said Sam was his idol. Now, he didn't care if he ever saw the boy, and would not hesitate to shoot him down if necessary. Larson only had room for one love in his heart, and she was here at his side.

"So, forget about him. All I want is you." He kissed her fingers.

Relieved, Carol leaned toward him. He put his arm around her. She rested her head on his shoulder.

"You were always the prettiest girl in Kansas," Larson said. "Men were always around you, but the first time I saw you, I knew we would be together."

"And everyone thought you were such a gentleman," she said softly. "But you were leading a double life."

"You never asked me to stop."

"I love you just as you are. I like sharing your secret."

He hugged her close and kissed her.

They didn't know that Leslie, pretending sleep, had stood up to stretch her legs. She had walked in a few circles and glimpsed them as the tarp sagged. She was unable to hear them but saw the obvious affection as they embraced and kissed with passion.

Sick at the sight, she went back to her spot against the rock. She sat down, fighting to keep the blankets around her as her hands had been retied in front of her. Somehow, she had to get out of there. She couldn't take the sickly Marianne, but she could bring back help. She didn't have any idea how to escape, but she was pinning her hopes on the nasty, always leering, Thatch.

*   *   *   *

That same moonlit night, at another camp far away in the lower hills to the east, Kansas and Billy rested. They had forded the Rio Grande a long time back and were deep in the wooded hills with a day's ride from the ranch. They had seen storm clouds and lightning strikes in the west.

Billy was finding it hard to converse with the ever-silent Kansas. He knew the gunfighter was their only hope against Larson, if the outlaw had survived the prison escape. Pa had said so. There was something about Kansas that made Billy feel connected, but he figured it was just because his father had wanted him found.

Billy's left arm still hurt, but he'd stopped wearing the sling. His burned right hand had peeling skin. He pushed more chips into the fire and wrinkled his nose at the smell.

Kansas, his wound high on his right shoulder healing well, felt no pain there, and his right fingers worked just fine, but his head still ached where he had been creased above his left ear. *How did I ever live this long?* Kansas asked himself. *Maybe because I'm needed here?* That one thought—being needed—was the only good one he'd had in years.

He also liked the clumsy kid with all his bravado.

"You'll like my pa," Billy said, abruptly.

Kansas, holding a cup of coffee, nodded as if disinterested.

"He's a great guy," Billy continued. "He never gets mad at anybody, not even me. Oh, he makes you feel guilty as heck if you do wrong. Just one look when he's disappointed in me, that hurts and it stays with me until I can do something better that makes him smile."

Staring into the fire, Kansas did not respond.

Billy sipped his coffee, made a face at the taste of it. "He's crazy about my ma. He buys her anything she wants. Like Paris dresses. And they hauled a rosewood piano all the way from Pennsylvania. She plays it real pretty."

Kansas liked the boy all the more but wished he would quiet down.

"Pa gave me some schooling, and wanted me to go to mining school. But I didn't want to be away from him. We spent a lot of time hunting and fishing. And getting cattle to market. So I talked him out of school, and now mostly I just read books." Billy hesitated. "And dime novels."

Again, no response from Kansas.

"But anyhow, way back in Kansas, when Pa saw my mother was getting letters from Larson when he was in prison, he had a fit. She said she had never encouraged Larson and was afraid of him. And then the last letter she got, Larson wrote he was going to bust out as soon as he could arrange it and come get her. We knew how Larson had broke out a couple times before, so Pa sold his business and moved us clear out of Kansas. All the way out here. Nobody knew where we were headed, not even friends. That was a year ago."

Kansas just waited, so Billy took out the novel with Kansas's image on the cover, holding it in the firelight, and continued.

"When Pa saw this, he got kind of excited, and right off, he sent me to find you, so I think he figured you could stop Larson." Billy shrugged. "But when I left the ranch, we didn't know about Larson's escape, or how he may be dead. But it don't matter, on account of there's no real proof of it, and they haven't pulled back on that big reward yet. Larson could still be out there and after my ma."

"Does he know where to find her?"

"Not so we knew about it, but Pa never stopped worrying."

Kansas set his cup aside, leaned back on his saddle, pulled his hat brim down. He closed his eyes but kept listening.

Billy rattled on. "I'll sure be glad when we get to the ranch. You'll like it there. We got the house all prettied up for Ma, but the barn needs a new roof. We got two hands can't speak a word of English, but they sure do a lot of work with the horses and cattle, and there's the old guy who makes things grow in the garden and takes the cook to town for supplies. I think he's got a thing for the cook."

Kansas listened and welcomed the chatter, because he was hurting, deep inside. Memories flashed of his younger, more innocent days, when he had studied for the ministry, and then the horror of war, but he avoided recalling all else because it was too painful.

41

*   *   *   *

That same night, back at the outlaw camp in the high ridges, Carol slept in blankets with her head on Larson's shoulder and his arm around her. Even with small pit fires and the larger cookfire, it was cold and damp. The tarps protected them from any drizzle, and the clouds were already moving south, revealing the moon and stars glistening in the dark sky.

The two captive women in their blankets, hands tied in front of them, were half hidden deep in the trees next to a tiny pit fire. Marianne, pale and ill, was a little worse by the hour.

Leslie fought to free her hands under her blanket. She kept trying even as her wrists started to bleed when the rawhide strings tightened, slowing her down. Now she had them bitten apart until they were loose enough to escape, but kept in place for show.

I'm getting out of here, Leslie thought. *Any way I can. But I have to go alone because Marianne would die out there. I have to get help somehow. Before they bury us.*

Leech, his aging body painful in the cold, was sitting on guard some distance from the women, and his head was down because he was sound asleep against a tree.

In a sheltered spot further away, Rumson's body lay covered with a blanket.

The Longley brothers slept off their whiskey. Target snored, off by himself. Turner was way down by the horses, on guard with his rifle, walking around to stay awake. He played his harmonica softly until his fingers nearly froze holding it. Even his face was stiff.

There was no sign of Charlie, who had not returned from breaking trail to the west. Moonlight and stars made it easy now to see all around the camp.

Leslie tensed as a dark shadow fell on her. She looked up at Thatch. She shriveled under his gaze. He was not wearing his gun belt. His intent was clear.

This was her chance. She didn't react to him.

He knelt, believing her hands were tied. He shoved a bandana in her mouth.

Leslie did not resist. She wanted to be away from the camp, whatever it took. He held his knife ready in case she fought him. When she didn't, he sheathed the blade at his belt. He yanked her to her feet, blankets and all. He threw her over his shoulder and marched off into the far trees, near where Rumson's body lay hidden under cover.

Leslie did not struggle. She was too busy freeing her hands. He took it as a sign that she was ready for him.

He moved into a dark clearing and threw her and her blankets onto the rough, rocky ground. He leered down at her as she lay quietly on her back.

Encouraged, he got down on his knees, straddling and hovering over her. She pretended to have her hands still bound by holding onto the rawhide strings.

Now he jerked the gag from her and suddenly his mouth was mauling hers. He tasted of tobacco and whiskey, making her stomach reel.

Her right hand fell on a nearby rock. Too small. She searched, found a big one.

With all her strength, she clobbered him on the head.

Thatch gasped, eyes wild. She hit him again. Unconscious, he fell on her. She fought to roll him aside and soon succeeded. She staggered to her feet and yanked one of the blankets until he rolled off, still unconscious.

Stay down, you dirty, old animal, she thought.

She took up the blanket, draped it around her. She dared

not try for a horse with Turner up and walking around them. She hurried through the trees, almost fell over Rumson's gear, which still lay near his covered body. Startled, she yet had the sense to take a roll of bread and a box of matches from the possible sack. She also untied the bedroll and took a slicker and another blanket. There was no weapon or canteen.

She drew the slicker on over her coat, and rolled the bread and matches into the blankets. She was forced to flee into the dark woods and brush, getting scratched every step of the way, and climbing haphazardly while trying to stay out of sight.

Hours passed in the night as she stumbled upward, reaching a dangerous height where the ground seemed to move under her boots. Wearing the slicker and carrying the blankets with the bread under her arm, she fought to get through brush and rocks, trying to keep her footing. Her aim was higher ground in the direction of the far distant trail they had traveled from the south. She needed to get her bearings and find her way to it.

"Dear God," she whispered. "Help me."

With dawn approaching in the outlaw camp, Leech woke up from guard duty. He sat up straight, could hardly move with his old bones complaining, but managed to get to his feet. He could see Turner way off by the horses, while the Longleys and Target slept in their blankets.

Leech stretched, turned to see Marianne sound asleep. And Leslie gone.

There was no sign of Thatch, so Leech figured he had Leslie off somewhere.

He turned to see Larson walking over.

And Larson was angry. "Where's the Texas woman?"

"I think Thatch took her off somewhere."

"And you let him?"

Leech winced. "I may have dozed off."

Larson, ready to explode, turned around as Thatch, head bloody, came staggering toward them. Thatch had a severe head wound and Larson could see he was in no mood for a tongue lashing.

"All right," Larson muttered to Thatch. "Where is she?"

"Gone. Ran off on foot." Thatch sat down, holding his head.

"I'll look," Leech offered, hurrying as fast as he could into the trees.

Fuming, Larson did see a plus. "At least I didn't hear her cry out."

"She didn't fight," Thatch grumbled. "She let me think it was okay, then she knocked me out with a rock. You just can't trust a woman."

Silent in his admiration for the Texas woman, Larson just shook his head. Utmost in his mind was Carol's reaction to whatever happened to the prisoners.

Leech returned after a few minutes. "No sign of her."

"Most likely, she'll die out there," Larson said.

"If she don't, she'll put the law on us," Leech complained. "She'll tell 'em who we are, and they'll know we didn't die in that avalanche."

"Maybe I should go after her," Thatch offered with a snarl.

"Never mind," Larson responded, a bit jittery at Leech's truth. "She can't get very far on foot. I'll just send Charlie after her when he returns."

Leech sat down by Thatch, who now had his head wrapped with a bandanna.

Thatch looked across the clearing at the sleeping Marianne. He wet his lips.

Larson, irritated by Thatch's animal needs, turned toward where Carol still slept.

*   *

High in the brush that early morning, just before dawn, Leslie faced a steep a terrain. She fought her way upward, wearing the slicker and carrying the bread in the rolled-up blankets. Her long hair lay damp and matted around her face and shoulders. She rested and savored a hunk of hard bread.

Aiming southeast, she was determined to get to the ranch, not even sure that anyone was still alive. It might take her a week on foot. Or longer, because of the clouds moving in overhead with the threat of more rain.

An unseen varmint scrambled through the nearby brush.

Now she faced another steep climb up and along the crest of a cliff. Worried the grade was saturated from the rain, there was no choice but to try. Halfway along, muddy earth began to move under her boots. She frantically grabbed at brush with her bare hands, but it was too late.

With a breathless cry, she went sliding down into a muddy mess. Wet and cold, she struggled to her feet and started back up the rocky climb. She was happy to find the hunk of bread still edible inside the blankets, but now she was thirsty and dazed with the knowledge that survival was not going to be easy.

CHAPTER FOUR

At Larson's camp in the high terrain at that same break of day, the sky was overcast with a rising wind. Occasional drizzle had begun. The cook fire was now protected by another tarp, enough to keep the fire going for the sickly prisoner.

Marianne, shivering as she sat by the crackling flames, was wrapped in a blanket. Carol huddled at her side. No one was in earshot.

"You need coffee," Carol told her as she sat by her. "And some breakfast."

"Where's Leslie?" Marianne murmured, grasping her cross.

"She ran away," Carol said gently. "Maybe she'll find her way home."

"I wish I could."

"No," Carol advised, "you wouldn't last a night out there."

"But what'll happen to me?"

"Nothing. Thorn knows you are my friend. He'll let you go when it's safe and not before."

"How do you know him? He's an outlaw."

"It's a long story, but trust me. You'll not be harmed."

"It's more than that, isn't it?"

"Marianne, don't worry, just get well."

Marianne, still in shock and feeling very ill, did not respond. She could only think of her husband's murder and how she would never see him again. He had been her true love, and the loss was close to unbearable. Tears often filled her eyes.

Carol believed Thorn meant no harm to her friends. She helped Marianne with another blanket but could see how feverish the woman was and how unlikely it was she would survive.

Seated close to the larger cookfire with Target, the women served themselves coffee and beans with his help. Target liked the ladies—any ladies.

When Larson came to check on them, Marianne fearfully avoided his gaze.

Carol leaned over to feel Marianne's brow. "Marianne, I think you have a real fever. You need to stay by the fire."

"I can't move anyway," Marianne whispered.

Larson wanted to say he cared but didn't, because Carol was all that really mattered to him.

An icy wind became more persistent despite the tarp, and at Carol's request, Target draped a slicker over Marianne. Then he added wood to the fire.

After a short while, Larson took Carol for a walk, away from the others, helping her keep her slicker up on her small shoulders. Her scarf now covered her hair.

She could tell he was heated up about something but all she could think of was Leslie, out there all alone, and Marianne's suffering. Still, she did not regret being there with Larson.

"Thorn, Marianne is very sick."

"She'll get better when the weather clears."

"And I'm so worried about Leslie."

"Don't be," Larson lied. "Charlie will find her and take her some place safe."

He led her to the rim of the terrain where they could see ahead to snowy peaks.

Still in agony after waking up from a nightmare just an hour before, Carol tried to seek comfort. "I dreamed about Sam last night."

"Forget him. Just tell me about Jack."

Carol, startled, stared up at him. "His kid brother? Why?"

Larson had been holding back on that part of his story, waiting for the right time, but then he had forgotten about it, and now he realized he had to tell her the rest of it.

"Who do you think put the law on me in the first place?"

"Jack? But he's so gentle," she said, bewildered. "He was studying to be a minister."

"Yeah, well, back then, someone told him how they saw us together one night in the hay loft."

"Oh, no," she whispered.

"He threatened to tell your folks if I didn't stay away from you."

"Did he?" she whispered, dismayed.

"No, I beat him to a pulp, so that scared him out of it." Larson sneered. "But then a week later, we hit the express office, just across the border. We wore masks like we always did."

Carol fought to keep silent and wait as he continued.

"We were leaving town in a hurry, but Jack was riding in and recognized my horse. He charged at me so hard, both our horses went down, and we hit the dirt in a heck of a fight. And that's how I got this scar on my face." Larson grimaced. "Thatch rode over and beat him on the head with a rifle butt, and I got back on my horse and we got going, but it was too late. The law was on us and tracked us down that same day."

"Why was Jack even there?"

"He must have followed us," Larson grunted. "But he's the reason I went to prison for the very first time."

"I didn't know."

"They never had my face or my name, or knew anyone in my gang, not before he got in the way. After we broke out, posters were everywhere. I ended up in prison time and again. Canon City was the last, till we busted out." Larson looked deadly. "I've waited all this time to make him pay, and he wasn't at the ranch, so where is he?"

"Oh, Thorn, he died in the war. In the second year. They even sent his Bible to Sam."

Angry, feeling deprived of his revenge, Thorn fell silent and walked back with her toward the cookfire. Carol knew now she had best say nothing more about Sam or his brother.

They reached the crackling fire where Marianne accepted more coffee from Target, just as the Ute came riding into camp. Carol sat beside her and took her hand, finding it cold and near frozen.

Charlie dismounted near the cookfire where he knelt to warm his hands.

Larson gestured to the Ute. "We need to talk."

Charlie poured himself some coffee, stood up and walked with Larson until they were in the trees and out of earshot.

Larson was still annoyed about Jack Cassidy having died in the war. He had been so thirsty for revenge, it had never occurred to him he would not get it. He tried instead to concentrate on the business at hand. "How's the trail ahead? Clear?"

Charlie nodded as he sipped his coffee.

"The Texas woman ran off on foot," Larson said. "You need to track her down and bring her back. We don't want her telling anyone who we are. And be sure to check for any signs of a posse while you're out there."

Charlie nodded. He knew Larson didn't really care what happened to Leslie, only that Carol must never blame him for it. Charlie, however, was more protective of women and hated being with the gang. Having been in prison for "borrowing" a lawman's horse, he had only wanted to get away far enough to be on his own and free of the law. Charlie had been promised a lot of money if he got them through the mountains alive and back to Larson's old hideout.

At that time, Charlie would break from them and head for home in northwestern Colorado, high in the Rockies where his wife and child were living with the tribe. Unsure he would receive promised payment for his services and end up alive, he might have to decide, instead, to take what he could, in advance, and run for it when the time came.

High in the rocky terrain the following day under a clear sky, Charlie found tracks in the mud that Leslie had not been able to cover. When he saw further signs heading southeast, he rode into the open. He hoped it would signal to the woman that he was here to help.

When he closed in on the area, he spotted her at the foot of the cliff. She was trying to crawl into the brush. Her clothes were torn, her hair matted, and her hands bleeding.

Charlie dismounted and walked toward to her. He put his hand over his heart as a sign of peace.

Leslie understood and let him come to her aid. He pulled her to her feet. She was caked with mud on her skirts and jacket. Shaken, hurting all over, she could hardly stand.

He helped her walk to shelter under an overhanging rock ledge. He brought blankets from his bedroll and wrapped them around her. Leslie had long ago lost her blankets and bread in a bad fall down a scree-covered slide which she had not been able to retrace. Charlie built a pit fire and made coffee. Grateful, she held her cup in both hands now, washed and bandaged, as he sat cross legged with his own cup.

"Now you will go home," he said.

Leslie, startled she would go free, broke into a big smile.

"Thank you," she said, as he nodded. "But then you'll be in trouble."

Charlie shook his head because he knew Larson needed him to cross the mountains and make it safely back to his secret hideout. Larson knew some of the landmarks but would never find them all without Charlie's help, and Charlie knew it.

Leslie enjoyed the hot coffee warming her inside. She felt safe around Charlie, and wondered how Marianne was, so she asked.

"Very sick," he said with a shrug and then eyed her bracelet. "I need to say you're dead."

Leslie winced. It had been her mother's, but Charlie was right. And Carol, for one, would never believe Leslie had given it up while still alive. It would serve as proof that she was dead.

Sick at heart, she removed the bracelet and handed it to him. "You're taking such a chance. Why?"

"You're a woman."

Leslie smiled at him with new admiration. Chivalry was expected down in Texas, but Charlie was proof it could be found anywhere.

"You must have a wife somewhere."

He almost smiled and then nodded. He gave her a small sack of food and matches. He had it in his mind to be on his way home before they could ever know she was still alive.

Now he had to return to Larson, and when Charlie rode away, Leslie wiped tears away.

She felt now that she did have a good chance of survival. She would follow the lower cliffs east until she recognized her home ground.

Meanwhile, on the trail back, Charlie suddenly became emotional with tears brimming. Helping Leslie had reminded him of how much he missed his loving wife, who would also praise him for saving Leslie.

To Charlie, women were as necessary as the sun. They were loving and kind. They bore children. They took care of their men. They did all the camp work. And they were always at your side when you were hurt. To sleep with her in his arms was a need that was driving him toward wanting to leave Larson at his very first chance.

Charlie knew the outlaws would have broken camp by now, though, so he was in no hurry. He would wait another night on his own before joining them. He wanted Leslie to have more time to find her way back. He sat staring into the crackling red and yellow flames as the night wore on, and it wasn't hard to picture his loving wife's smile.

* * * *

Reaching the Cassidy Ranch on a late and dreary afternoon, Kansas and Billy approached slowly from the south. They saw no activity, not even up at the corrals, but out of caution, they reined to a halt some distance east of the house.

In front of the garden gate, a saddled white mule was standing along with two sorrel horses at the hitching rail.

"Oh, no," Billy said. "That's Finnegan's mule."

Kansas didn't respond but saw how nervous the youth acted.

"Don't believe anything he says about me," Billy pleaded. "Sure, I roped and dragged off his necessary, but how was I supposed to know he was in it? It was the middle of the night, for gosh sakes. And I didn't really run off his old mule. It followed me. For a handful of grain, but..."

Kansas fought back a smile and thought, *There was a time when I would have given anything to have a son like this.*

Billy had a foolish look on his face. "Yeah, okay, so it gets boring out here, and I had to have something fun to do. And heck, he sung in the choir at our Sunday go meetings, so I figured he wouldn't kill me, no how."

Kansas fought to keep a straight face, but now they both saw a little dog running downhill from the barn toward the house. It had black and brown spots on a white fluffy coat. A mongrel mix, it had floppy ears and a busy tail, along with big dark brown eyes.

"Yikes," Billy said, reining to a halt. "He's got Bonnie with him."

Kansas drew back on the reins, waiting.

"That little dog takes on everything and everybody. Skunks, snakes, cougars, and anything up to ten times her size. She thinks she's a heck of lot bigger than she really is. And she don't like anybody, except Miss Leslie."

They rode on at a walk as they saw the dog enter the garden in front of the house.

"He uses her to hunt," Billy added. "She's got a good nose."

Soon they reined up again, still at some distance, but with a better view of the hills beyond the house.

"Things don't look right," Billy said.

Frenzied all of a sudden, Billy dug in his heels and rode ahead of Kansas, who followed behind, but more cautiously.

When they reached the mule at the hitching rail, they reined up short.

Bonnie came running forward and charged the gate, staying safely behind it as she barked at them. The horses ignored her. She was so small compared to the world she wanted to eat up, it tickled Kansas. He figured she'd take on a grizzly.

Out of the house came a husky, tall Black man with thin mustache, trim beard, and dangerous eyes. Middle-aged, good-looking, he wore a long, dark coat, wide-brimmed hat, and a bright blue bandanna. He was also wearing a side arm.

"Mr. Finnegan," Billy called.

Finnegan came down and through the garden gate, Bonnie at his heels. She growled and barked, but stayed behind him, and then sat and went silent.

"Mr. Finnegan, this is my friend, Kansas Red."

Finnegan had heard of Kansas—and his reputation—but didn't respond.

"Where's my pa?" Billy asked, frantic.

Finnegan gestured over his left shoulder. They now saw the four new graves on the slope between the house and barn, marked by wooden crosses and fresh red and white flowers.

"Four days ago. Your pa. Mr. Walker. And two hands. All dead," Finnegan said. "The cook and the old man who drove her, they couldn't get back from town until after the hail storm, and when they found everyone here, they had to come over to my ranch for help. Both of them were so broken up, they've left for good. Same for the housekeeper when she heard about it. They won't be back."

Kansas looked down so that his hat brim hid the pained look on his face.

Billy gasped, shaken, "My mother, where is she?"

"They took her, and Miss Leslie, and Mrs. Walker, too."

Billy winced, tears in his eyes. "But who done it?"

"No one knows."

"Had to be Thorn Larson," Billy said. "He was after my ma."

Finnegan shook his head. "I heard he died in the mountains. Weeks ago. Buried under twenty feet of snow, the paper said."

"It had to be him," Billy insisted, angrily wiping the tears from his face.

"Even if he is still alive," Finnegan asked, "why would he

come all the way down here? Why not escape to California or down to Mexico instead?"

"I told you, he was after my mother."

Finnegan followed Billy's gaze to the barn where two men were coming out of the side door. "My hands. Folks been taking turns here."

"Was there a posse?" Billy asked.

"Not that we could see. There was no trail because of the storm," Finnegan said. "Heavy with hail so big, it dug holes in the ground. It dragged on for days. The wind tore down trees in the hills. Mud slides and a flash flood. By the time it was over, there were no tracks anywhere. In any direction." Finnegan paused to spread his coat aside from his left, revealing a star on his vest. "Sheriff deputized me just in case any of 'em come back this way."

Billy stared a moment at the shiny badge that read Deputy Sheriff.

"Sorry, Billy," Finnegan offered.

"Pa said you prospected in the mountains west of here," Billy said, fresh tears flowing. "You know all the trails. You've even brought us arrowheads you found in the caves around there, so you know where they can hide."

"Yes, but we found no signs that they headed west," Finnegan insisted. "They could have just as well gone in any direction. I heard of a small posse headed west out of Pueblo, but they turned back in the storm. Our sheriff seems to be waiting to see if the women turn up to give us direction."

Billy choked on his tears. He knew Finnegan meant "bodies" of the women. He turned his horse suddenly and rode over to the graves where he dismounted to kneel, hat in hand. It was approaching twilight and gloomy.

Kansas wanted badly to go with Billy, to comfort him in this terrible moment, but instead, he dismounted, hiding his own reaction behind his horse. Finally, he walked around the roan and faced Finnegan at the hitching rail. They were appraising each other.

Bonnie sniffed at Kansas but didn't bark. In fact, she wagged her tail. She stood on her hind legs and clawed at Kansas legs in an effort to be picked up. Failing, she dropped down and ran in circles.

"Heard about you," Finnegan said to Kansas.

"Billy told me about some troubles he caused you in the past."

Finnegan nodded with a half smile. "Yeah, he's full of the devil sometimes. Got no other young folks around, so he has to make his own mischief. But I held a shotgun on him until he got my outhouse back in business."

Finnegan sobered as he followed Kansas's gaze toward the graves.

"How many were there?" Kansas asked.

"I saw signs of maybe eight to ten horses in front of the house, but not so you could tell which direction they went. The hail took care of that."

"We'll head west," Kansas said. "I figure if they went in any other direction out of here, they'd have been spotted at some point in time."

"Want me with you?"

"Yes."

Finding himself unable to control his emotions, Kansas struggled with his words. "I'll check on Billy."

His own eyes watering now, Kansas left his mount at the rail and walked the distance to the graves. He stood next to Billy, who rose, tightly gripping his hat, his face was wet with tears. Neither spoke for a time. Then Billy turned and, leading his horse, walked back toward the house.

Kansas hesitated, crossed his heart, murmured a prayer, and turned to follow.

It was then that Billy gathered himself up, his tears replaced by burning anger by the time they were back with Finnegan. "When are we leaving?"

"Daybreak." Finnegan pushed his hat back. "We'll need plenty of grub. Pack horse, extra mounts. A good supply of grain. All the firearms and shells you have in the house. A lot of blankets. Gets cold up there. And wet."

"We still got horses?" Billy asked, looking toward the barn.

"Yes, they didn't bother with 'em," Finnegan said. "In too much of a hurry."

"Which way will we go?" Billy persisted.

"West," Kansas said.

Finnegan nodded. "But we'll need something from Miss Leslie," Finnegan said. "For Bonnie."

Billy hesitated. "Yeah, okay, one of her scarves."

"And something of your mother's," Finnegan added. "I'll tell my men to send word to the sheriff we're headed west. Just to give him a head's up."

Billy looked warily at Kansas. He wanted to say he had no money to pay the gunman, but by now, Billy had the sense to know Kansas would be offended by any offer.

Traveling with him, Billy had learned there was even more to Kansas Red than anyone may have thought. And now he could see that the man was also incensed by the raid, maybe out of chivalry for the women, but possibly for justice itself. Or just maybe, there was a big reward for Larson... But Billy discounted even that thought.

Billy mounted his horse and reached over as Kansas handed him the reins of his roan. Bonnie barked at Billy while wagging her tail. Ignoring her, Billy headed for the barn and corrals.

Bonnie barked after him as if she had chased him away.

Kansas and Finnegan watched Billy meet up with Finnegan's ranch hands.

"Tough on the boy," Finnegan muttered.

Later that night in the house, after a hastily prepared supper and with a fire in the hearth, Finnegan sat down at the rosewood piano to play a hymn. Bonnie hid behind his feet and barked once at Billy, wagging her tail, then finally curled up and slept.

"That dog hates me," Billy said.

"She just wants you to play with her," Finnegan mused, his fingers moving gently on the keyboard.

"Yeah, that why she always wants to bite my boots?" Billy got out of his chair and yawned. "There's a cot in my father's office. I'll sleep there."

After Billy left, Finnegan continued to play.

Kansas got up from the couch and walked to the fireplace to stoke the fire. He saw a collection of old tintypes and later photographic images on the mantle. All were framed and none were less than eight inches tall. A gold frame held a closeup of Carol, down to her waist, in her wedding gown, holding a bouquet of flowers. He could picture her on the steps of the church with Sam.

Could she really have chosen Larson above anyone else?

He walked back to the couch and sat down facing the coffee table where he now set about cleaning their collected rifles and revolvers. Bonnie peered at him from behind Finnegan's feet.

Kansas admired Leslie's Winchester 73, which was inscribed: *Grand Prize July 4, 1875, Leslie Allen, Champion Sharpshooter, Forth Worth, Texas.*

Finnegan continued playing hymns but not singing. Bonnie just lay at his feet while watching Kansas, as if making a judgment.

Finnegan stopped between hymns. "You have a wife, Kansas?"

"No."

"Lost mine in childbirth. Both of them."

Kansas could see the ongoing grief and respected the man for his obvious strength and fortitude.

"Bonnie is named after her," Finnegan said, as he tickled the keys and studied Kansas. He could see concern in the gunman's dark gaze, but he also caught a glimpse of Kansas wiping his eyes with the back of his hand.

After a time, Finnegan began to play "Tenting Tonight on the Old Campgrounds," a ballad that had reached the hearts of men on both sides of the war, and now he sang softly:

"Many are the hearts that are weary tonight,
Waiting for the War to cease,
Many are the hearts that are looking for the light,
To see the dawn of peace."

Finnegan's voice was soft and deep, almost putting Kansas to sleep. Both men had been in the War Between the States on the side of the Union. Both had memories, painful and better forgotten, but the song was one of hope for all who had suffered and survived.

And now perhaps, hope that they would find the women alive. A fragile wish.

After Finnegan stopped playing altogether, Kansas stretched out on the couch, lying on his back and closing his eyes. He was half asleep when something heavy landed on his belly. He jerked awake and stared at Bonnie, who settled on top of him with her eyes already closed.

Kansas looked at Finnegan, who grinned.

"I've never seen her do that with anyone she didn't know,"

Finnegan said, a little dismayed. "I think you passed inspection, but it won't be for sure until the time comes that you wake up to the gift of a dead mouse."

Kansas gave in and went to sleep with Bonnie dozing on his belly. He had a restless night with nightmares that once sent a tear down his cheek. He was awakened before dawn by Bonnie busily licking his face.

"Yeah," he muttered, "I like you, too, but take it easy, will you?"

Bonnie hesitated long enough to listen, then quickly went back to washing his face for him as he hurriedly got up to escape.

*   *   *   *

After waiting another day to give Leslie more time, Charlie arrived at the current outlaw camp in the hills. It was twilight under a clear sky. It was icy cold and there were patches of snow.

Charlie dismounted and walked over to the campfire where Carol stood with Larson. He handed the bracelet to Larson, who gave it to the tearful Carol, who then sat down haphazardly to suffer with the loss.

"She would never part with this, ever," Carol whispered. "Not if she were alive."

Larson turned to Charlie and for Carol's benefit asked, "You give her a decent burial?"

Charlie nodded and turned away.

Carol sobbed and stroked the bracelet. She felt sorry for her friend, but even then, her own interests took precedent as she convinced herself she was blameless. She wanted to be with the only man she had ever loved. She wanted pretty things, comfort, and to be admired by all. Yes, she grieved for Leslie, but not above her own needs.

Larson knelt beside her and took her hand.

"I'm so sorry for Leslie," Carol said, wiping her eyes. "I don't think I'll tell Marianne."

It was then that Target walked over to the fire with a cup of coffee, which he set down by the pot. "Your friend Marianne just died."

Carol burst into tears. Yet later, after she had handled the loss of both friends, she realized it had been inevitable. No one was to blame, she told herself.

The next day, at the break of dawn with clouds moving in, Larson arranged the burial of Marianne Walker. The grave was deep in the trees with a wooden cross of limbs and was covered with rocks to keep it safe.

Carol lingered behind while the men went back to break camp. She made sure no one was around to see her actions. She secretly drew Marianne's little gold cross from her jacket and dangled it on the wooden cross. She knew Larson would have stopped her, but she owed that much to her friend. She thought surely no one would find the grave or know the meaning of the cross.

"I'm sorry, Marianne," she whispered.

Now she hesitated only a moment before taking out Leslie's bracelet. She glanced around once more to be sure no one knew what she was doing, and she put the bracelet at the foot of the cross. She would later tell Larson she had thrown both items away because they were painful reminders. She would assure him they were deep in brush where they would not be found. She felt safe because she could not imagine anyone finding the grave or knowing who lay there.

Rising, she walked back through the trees.

Larson remained kind to her during her grief, but as time went on, she became bright again, looking forward to all of his promises.

*   *   *   *

Further east and still high in the rocky terrain, Leslie had new hope she could make it back alive. That night, weary, torn, and exhausted, she finally slept in a cave with a tiny fire.

Days later, she was still stumbling along the ridge, staying high so she could have a view of the terrain and any danger. Her skirts were torn at the hem. She ached all over.

The ground under her boots was muddy and rocks slid as she moved.

Now just before twilight, she spotted the make-shift posse moving towards her on the trail, but barely distinguishable in the fading light. She gasped as she recognized the white mule in the lead.

"Mr. Finnegan," she whispered.

In a great hurry to reach them, she became careless on the downward path. Rocks rolled aside. Brush was scarce, and the ground was soft from the recent storm.

The side of the ridge began to move under Leslie's feet with a sudden roar. She cried out and tried to grab at a clump of brush but failed. The whole side of the rise was falling away.

She was lifted and dragged and thrown like a rag doll, carried down in a river of moving, wet earth, unable to seize anything but falling rocks.

Carried down, helpless, she called out with a wavering voice, knowing she would not be heard.

As she careened to a flat spot below, rocks hit her body and then her head.

She was unconscious the rest of the way down.

CHAPTER FIVE

The roar of the slide on the ridge startled the small posse on the trail below as it rode forward in the twilight. They saw a high-ridge chunk of earth come crashing down, carrying rocks and brush.

Trailing his friends, Billy led two spare horses and a pack horse. He reined up in dismay. "I saw somebody," he called out. "Somebody falling."

Kansas and Finnegan, with Bonnie in front of him on the saddle, left Billy behind as they rode up the steep grade to have a look at the slide further along the cliff.

They reined up and watched as the side of the rise shifted and roared once more, hurtling a huge rock down a gully, unaware it had just missed the fallen Leslie.

As Finnegan rode up closer to the slide, Bonnie got agitated and tried to get down. Finnegan held her as he dismounted and then set her on the rocky ground. She took off toward the far edge of the slide and near a heap of brush away from it.

Bonnie disappeared in the rocks and brush, but was suddenly barking frantically.

As Finnegan searched the rough terrain, he found Bonnie

licking Leslie's face so franticly that Leslie opened her eyes and managed a smile before passing out again. He knelt and carefully searched for broken bones, getting no pained reaction.

Kansas rode up and dismounted, wary of the slide.

Seeing Finnegan on his knees in the brush, Kansas left his roan ground-tied near the mule. He walked forward just as Finnegan stood up with an unconscious woman in his arms. A beautiful woman with long, flaxen hair. Torn clothing. Blood on her hands and left cheek.

"It's Miss Leslie," Finnegan said. "I don't think anything's broken. Here, you take her. I'll look around, see what I find."

Kansas panicked. *No, not me, God, no.*

Finnegan handed Leslie over to the startled Kansas, who had never held a good woman in his arms. He stood frozen as Finnegan brushed off her clothes and hair. With her head on his right shoulder and her skirt-covered legs over his left arm, Kansas felt more fear than he had ever felt in the war or a gun fight. Holding her was devastating. He took tentative steps, desperate to unload her someplace really soon.

Finnegan looked around the brush area and the slide but found nothing that might belong to her. He returned to the nervous Kansas.

"She has a head injury," Finnegan said as he picked up Bonnie. "I'll bring your horse. Just watch your step going down."

As Finnegan led the mule and horse down around him, Kansas felt like he was carrying a load of dynamite. He fretted every inch of the way, certain he would lose his footing and drop her. A tough gunfighter acting like a fool. Even injured, she was soft and lovely, and too traumatic a load for him.

Worried sick, Kansas slowed his descent as much as he could down the steep grade.

Part way down, she opened her eyes and looked up at him.

She slid her left arm up his chest and neck, and held on as she again closed her eyes.

Don't die on me, Kansas pleaded silently.

Waiting at the foot of the grade with the spare horses and pack horse, Billy caught sight of her, and had a happy grin. Someone was alive! That gave him hope for his mother.

Finnegan brought down the other horses while Bonnie jumped free and ran ahead.

"Don't set her down yet," Finnegan said to Kansas. "I remember there's a shallow cave around the bend, just ahead. We'll make camp there, see what we can do for her."

Following Finnegan, Kansas was still convinced he might drop her. Eyes closed, she clung to him and even shifted in his arms. She wasn't that light, but she was soft. Soft and warm. A shattering experience for Kansas, it didn't fit with his hard, bounty-hunting life.

He followed Finnegan to the half-cave, then waited for blankets to be spread against an upturned saddle. He set her down as carefully as he could and stepped back, while Finnegan covered her up and Bonnie finished washing her face, at which point Leslie opened her eyes briefly, then closed them again.

Billy gathered wood and chips while Kansas loosened cinches and tethered the horses in the nearby trees. They built a crackling fire and made coffee as night fell.

As Bonnie rose from her lap and licked her nose, Leslie, leaning back against the saddle, opened her eyes and managed a flickering smile. Billy struggled to hold back his questions while Finnegan checked her vision and felt her face and brow for fever.

"You were real fortunate," Finnegan said.

"I prayed all the way down," she whispered.

Finnegan worried. "That's a bad bruise on your left temple. Try to stay upright until morning."

She nodded, closing her eyes again and seeming to fade once more. Bonnie settled in her lap.

Kansas watched in silence, awed by how lovely she was, despite her injuries. He stood back out of the firelight so he could more easily watch her and still stand guard. Firelight danced on her golden hair.

Billy got excited when she again opened her eyes. He knelt close to her.

"Miss Leslie," Finnegan said. "That's Kansas Red. And you know Billy."

"Where's my mother?" Billy asked. "Is she okay?"

Leslie, handed a cup of coffee by Finnegan, held it in her shaky hands. She couldn't tell Billy that his mother went so willingly with Larson.

"Yes," Leslie whispered. "But Marianne was very sick when I left."

"Who were the raiders?" Finnegan asked.

"Thorn Larson," she said, sipping the coffee. "And some other really bad men."

"I knew it," Billy muttered.

"How did you get away?" Finnegan persisted.

"One of them dragged me off into the trees, and I hit him with a rock. I ran away. Charlie, a Ute Indian, was sent to bring me back, but he helped me so I could have a chance to find my way home. He even took my mother's bracelet to show them to prove I was dead."

"Where are they headed?" Finnegan asked.

"All I know is they are going west. Some hideout where Larson's meeting his cousins who are supposed to be bringing some gold they are going to share. I could see snow on the mountains in the direction they were headed."

"And how many are there with Larson?"

"Aside from Charlie, there were six, and one more who died."

"Can we catch up with them?" Billy asked, worried and afraid.

"I don't know," she said, still confused with a headache. "It's been several days."

Finnegan gave her a very small plate of hot beans, and she ate hungrily.

"Did you see any sign of a posse?" he asked.

"No," she said as Bonnie tried to nestle even more under the plate she was balancing. She glanced toward Kansas, a dark figure out of firelight. Now she put her hand to her brow and her eyes fluttered.

"Maybe you'd better sleep," Finnegan said. "But don't lie down."

He had barely spoken when she slid down a little further, but was still mostly upright against the saddle. She closed her eyes with Bonnie shifting position on her lap.

A restless Billy finally returned to his blankets and slept out of pure exhaustion.

Kansas stood up and walked into the trees with Finnegan following. They spoke low, out of earshot, in the cold of the starry night.

"That's one tough lady," Finnegan said. "Tougher than that boy over there."

"Billy?"

"Yeah, Sam would have given his life for him." Finnegan adjusted his hat. "Maybe we all would have. But the more Sam loved the boy, the less his mother seemed to. Now it's tearing the kid apart that she's all he has left."

Kansas stared into the night. *You have to be wrong*, he thought. *Every mother loves her child.*

"I'll take first watch," Finnegan said.

Kansas nodded and went back into the firelight where Billy slept in his blankets.

He spread his own bedroll, but before he could kneel down, he discovered Leslie watching him while Bonnie slept in her lap. Finnegan was out of hearing and Billy was deep in slumber.

Kansas moved to kneel near her and spoke softly. "You need to rest. You had a bad fall." He pulled the blankets higher and tucked them around her.

"I'm worried," she said, speaking in whispers. "For Billy."

Kansas didn't respond but he listened intently.

"His mother's with Larson," she whispered.

"You mean she's his prisoner?"

"No, I mean she's *with* him."

Kansas did not want to believe her. "Maybe she's just trying to survive."

"I think Billy should go back."

"He'll never do that," Kansas said, feeling her brow. "And you won't get through tomorrow unless you sleep tonight. But remember, stay upright."

She hunkered down just a little as Bonnie shifted her position.

"Close your eyes," he said.

"I'm afraid if I do, I may not wake up. Unless I hold your hand."

A little shaken and surprised, Kansas nodded. He thought *this will only take a short while.* He sat near her right side, sharing the edge of the saddle, and because he was so much taller, he hovered over her. She gripped his strong left hand with her right and then slowly slid her fingers inside his palm, but it wasn't enough for her comfort.

Before she fell asleep, she wrapped her right arm around his left and gripped his hand again. He thought once she slept, he would be able to move away, but each time, she would awaken.

He finally found a comfortable position, still sharing the edge of the saddle. He let her cling to his arm and hand, which she clutched to her side. He looked down at her in kindness as he thought back to his youthful study for the ministry, nearly eighteen years ago. After the life he had led since, he was a stranger, even to himself, but he worried over her as if he had been a man of the cloth. He refused to think it was because he felt a deep attraction.

After a while, Finnegan came for coffee and to change guard. He looked down at Kansas sitting near Leslie with her arm through his and his hand clamped in hers. Both were upright and asleep against the upturned saddle, with Bonnie still on her lap. The whole scene was peaceful. A gunfighter and bounty hunter imprisoned by a beautiful Texas lady.

Finnegan had to grin as he added wood to the fire.

Leslie, sleeping soundly, had nestled even nearer to Kansas, her head on his upper arm while still holding tight to his hand. As Leslie turned more on her side, Bonnie shifted to stay in place but failed, so she jumped over onto Kansas's lap, which startled him awake.

Kansas tried to sit up as Finnegan lay blankets over them both.

Finnegan smiled. There was no way he wanted to disturb the gentle scene.

Moving his lips in a call for help, Kansas appealed to Finnegan, who just shook his head. They both knew Leslie might have a serious head injury. It was also obvious this was not Kansas's usual occupation.

For guard duty, Finnegan would call on Billy, but he could not help grinning to himself.

*   *   *   *

That same night in a mountain camp at a far distance ahead, the outlaws felt it was safe to build a larger campfire, especially with snow hanging on the peaks and being surrounded by banks that hid any view of them.

Carol sat in the circle of Larson's arm as they shared coffee away from the others at a separate fire of their own. It was obvious to everyone who saw them together that they were in love. Not only now, but with a history.

"I'm sorry about my friends," Carol said, as she brushed dirt from her satin skirts and frowned at her dress, "but I've been wearing this old rag until it itches."

"Don't worry," he said, "you'll have so many dresses, you'll need a dozen closets."

She leaned against him, staring into the firelight.

They were silent awhile, but he had more on his mind. "Will you miss the boy?"

"Yes, of course, but we were never close. He was always crazy about Sam. They spent all their time together. Hunting and fishing. I was never a big part of Billy's life."

"So you can turn your back on him?"

"Yes. I have to, Thorn, or he would try to take revenge on you."

Larson was irritated but quiet as she closed her eyes.

*   *   *   *

Back in the posse's camp in the shallow cave, it would be long after midnight before Kansas could slip free of the sleeping Leslie's grip and roll aside. Bonnie spilled from his lap and climbed back in Leslie's.

Kansas gathered his blankets and got to his feet. Finnegan slept on the other side of the fire pit, with Billy off with the horses and on guard.

Kansas began to realize he missed being with Leslie at his side. He had spent his life with no loved one to care if he came or went—or if he lived or died. Now his arms felt so empty, his eyes misted. Where had he gone so wrong? He knew why but had let it happen unawares.

Stoking the fire and adding chips, then rolling in his blankets, Kansas had trouble falling asleep. Although Leslie's unusually strong grip had held his arm and shoulder in a cramped position, he was painfully reminded that he was ever a lonely man.

As he lay restless in his bedding, Kansas stared out at the shifting clouds and bright stars.

He felt it was far too late to change. He was also losing heart at the way he was.

Early morning, Leslie awakened to find herself hurting but with clear vision and thought. She sat up with Bonnie shifting around in her lap on top of her blankets. She looked over beyond the fire to see Billy asleep while Finnegan was making breakfast.

She could see Kansas off on the slope with the horses.

It took a moment to recall that she had gone to sleep holding his hand. She remembered being afraid she would not wake up without holding onto someone. Now as she looked at the strange combination of gunfighter and comforter, she had only one thought: *You have to be a Texan at heart.*

Still with a headache and hurting all over, she lifted Bonnie from her lap and set her aside. She got to her knees, then faltered and sat back down.

Finnegan came over with a cup of coffee and spoke in a low voice. "Stay put, and when you are ready to move, make it very slow."

"Are you a doctor?" she asked softly.

"No, but I did my time in the war. We had to help each other."

Keeping her voice quiet, she nodded toward Kansas. "What kind of a man is he?"

"I figure he's about as deadly as a man can get and still have kindness of heart. That's all I know, so far."

"Is he married?"

Finnegan shrugged. "No, and I doubt he ever will be."

"Want to bet?"

With a chuckle, Finnegan just shook his head.

Leslie sipped her coffee as Bonnie moved back into her lap.

With bright sunlight, Kansas returned for breakfast as Billy awakened.

Billy moved to pour himself some coffee. "Miss Leslie, you look a lot better."

She nodded. "Everything hurts. But I'm okay now."

"We can give you a horse to head back to the ranch and spread the word," Finnegan added. "Or you can come with us."

"I'm riding with you," she said.

"We have your rifle on the pack saddle," Finnegan opened a can of beans and dumped them into a pan. "There's a trading post on the way, if it's still there. We can get you outfitted."

"In the middle of nowhere?"

Finnegan nodded. "Grossman's. Sits on the creek trail that runs north to the mines. They outfit mule trains to the diggings and gold trains back down and south to the border. Even the army travels that road. Both he and his wife are getting on in years, but last time I was there, they said they were going to hire a few hands."

While the horses were being saddled, Billy and Leslie were alone for a short while by the now-smothered fire, seated with the last of the coffee. She could see he was troubled.

"I'm sure your mother will be okay," she said.

73

"I never told her I loved her."

"Mothers always know."

"And my pa, I never told him how much I cared."

"Yes, you did," she replied. "Every time you were at his side."

Billy stood up and wiped his eyes.

"What do you really know about Kansas?" she asked.

Billy reached inside for the dime novel and pulled it out to show her.

"Oh, my," she responded. "It looks just like him."

"Yeah, and my pa sent me to get him to help us."

"He certainly looks mean enough," she said as he slid the novel back into his coat.

"Yeah, but Pa always said, no man is so tough a woman can't make him plain silly."

"Your father was a very wise man." Seeing new tears in his eyes, Leslie hurriedly changed the subject. "I noticed your horse is limping."

"Yeah, maybe a stone bruise, so I've got to saddle up a spare."

Later that morning under a cloudy sky, the little posse came upon the abandoned outlaw camp with Rumson's grave, which Bonnie promptly found. Leslie knew it was him because of the location, right on the same spot where he died.

"I think he was already dying," she said, "and I heard Thatch say Larson had finished him off with a knife."

Billy panicked. "And my mother is with them?"

"She's safe," Leslie assured him.

Early the next day, the sun was shining as they traveled west. They rode through rocks and trees but reined up because Bonnie started to squirm in front of Finnegan on his saddle. He tried to calm her.

But Bonnie began barking and looking into the brush on their right.

Kansas, scouting ahead and off in the trees to their left, turned his mount around, then stopped where he could look back and see Bonnie.

Billy, behind Finnegan, ahead of Leslie, looked frantically around.

Bonnie kept barking and trying to leap free of Finnegan.

All of a sudden, they all froze.

A large female skunk, trailed by six half-grown youngsters, came out of the brush. Undaunted and acting as if the mule was just more tree trunks, the female crossed right between the legs of Finnegan's mount. Had he been on a horse, it might not have ended so well.

Behind Finnegan, Billy's horse snorted and danced a little at the smell. Further back, Leslie's mount tossed its head and sidled back a few steps.

All held their breath, but the mule did not budge. Unfazed by the barking, the mother and youngsters continued from under the mule's belly and into the brush on the other side of the trail. The smelly skunks waddled through the briars until they were finally out of sight.

Kansas only got a glimpse of them, having stayed ahead in the trees.

The travelers breathed a collective sigh of relief. Bonnie finally stopped barking and they continued on. Soon Kansas returned and rode behind Finnegan as they moved along, single file.

A day later, they came on to another abandoned camp where Bonnie went wild on Finnegan's saddle once again. He stepped down with her and she immediately jumped from his arms. The others dismounted, and all followed the little dog to Marianne's grave which was deep in a stand of tall aspens.

A shattered Leslie knelt by the wooden marker with the little gold cross, but left it intact as tears filled her eyes. She retrieved her mother's bracelet.

Leslie wondered how Carol had managed to leave the jewelry, since she was sure Larson would have stopped her. But Leslie was grateful Carol had found a way. She slid the bracelet onto her left wrist.

Billy was mumbling to himself, worried that if Marianne had passed away on the journey, maybe his mother might also fall along the harsh trail.

*   *   *   *

While the small posse continued westward, days ahead was the trading post, set deep in a wide clearing, bordered on the north and south by rough heights. It faced formidable mountains with snow crested ridges to the west beyond a southbound creek.

The post was about to be invaded by the outlaws in broad daylight.

A combination of house, store, and mining supplier in one long building, it also had a back area with a barn and corrals, offering mules and horses. It was set on the east side of the wide, shallow but swiftly-flowing Grossman's Creek. The water ran from the mines in the north, rushing south toward New Mexico Territory with canyon walls before and after the post location. A wide, mostly elevated road on the east side of the creek served the mule trains in both directions, north and south.

To the far west, a red rock formation could be seen standing in the high mountains like a sentinel. To reach that point from the creek involved crossing nearly impossible terrain with scattered pines, brush, and rocky barriers.

A bumpy wagon road, running from the east, ended in front of the post because, across the creek to the west, the terrain was nearly impassable. Coming from the Rio Grande to the post, the road was often blocked in narrow passes by avalanches and mud slides, which made it unsuitable for any large amount of traffic.

When Larson and his gang approached from the north cliffs, a mule train had just moved out of sight to the south. All seemed quiet and serene at the post.

The outlaws moved in on the post with little warning or fanfare.

Larson greeted the elderly Grossmans in a friendly manner. He learned that no more mule trains were expected for another ten days, and supplies from the wagon road, not for two weeks. No military or law were in the area.

Then the outlaws took over. Gold dust in sacks and a few handfuls of gold and silver coins were taken from the safe. Larson took possession of the sacks, but he allowed the coins to be shared among his men. He promised to share the dust at the hideout, along with the gold his cousins were bringing.

"There'll be plenty to go around," Larson promised.

Out at the corrals, Thatch and the Longleys accosted the two old hands—both former mule-skinners and prospectors— guarding them as they fed and watered the horses and mules. Fresh mounts would be taken and stone-sore outlaw ponies, like Larson's pinto, would be left behind.

Charlie, about to ride west to scout a trail, chose a chunky bay and saddled it. He added his gear, a good supply of food and shells, and a full canteen.

As Charlie forded the creek and rode out of sight, the old timers were herded to the main building where they joined the elderly Grossmans only long enough for a meal. This continued for the length of their stay, all to impress upon Carol that no one would be harmed. One of the outlaws was always on guard at the barn.

Carol and Larson were seldom seen outside the back rooms. There, in privacy, Larson would repeat his promises. "You'll the be queen of South America."

"And you'll be king," she said, kissing his cheek.

In the public rooms, the elderly owners, Wally and Tina Grossman, both grey-haired and lame, were forced to do the outlaws' bidding for several days. Tina had to do the cooking and Wally served food at the tables near the kitchen.

Thatch, Leech, and the Longleys often spent their time drinking on the front porch.

Target and Turner, both with huge appetites, hovered around Mrs. Grossman, a sweet old lady in a pink-flowered apron, whenever she was cooking. To her amusement, they ate any and everything in sight. Both she and her husband saw no reason to fear these two buffoons. When no one was in earshot, they questioned both men as they ate more slices of apple pie.

"Don't you boys have something better to do with your lives?" Mrs. Grossman asked softly.

"We tried everything else," Target said, looking foolish. "We was no good at herding cows. We can't read or write. We tried prospecting, but we never found a single nugget. Then we tried cattle rustling and got caught right in the middle of it."

"You know," she whispered, "there are big diggings up north. Lots of gold."

Target and Turner were interested but could see no way to take advantage.

Meanwhile, Larson and Carol were still enjoying private rooms at the post where she could have a hot bath and help herself to a storeroom full of women's clothes.

"Not very fancy," she complained of the soft gingham colors.

"Our time will come," Larson assured her.

Only feeling beautiful when adorned with luxury, Carol shuddered at the feel of the crisp fabrics. Larson, ever amused at her show of vanity, didn't know that she had no self-confidence, no feeling of worth without silk, ribbons, and lace.

At one point, she drew a sheet of lace from a shelf, hoping it would be a wedding veil. He had promised her there was a mission on the way where they could be married.

Nights, after Carol retired with Larson, the post occupants would be kept in the cooking area where they could have the heat of the stove and be under guard.

But Carol worried about Mrs. Grossman. "She's so nice to me. Will they be okay?"

He sat on the bed with her and hugged her. "Why do you think I told them we were going south along the creek? So if a posse shows, that's what these folks will tell them."

"They won't wonder if we went west instead?"

"No one would even think we could tackle those mountains."

"Will it be safe? They look so…"

"Don't worry, we have that Indian to get us through it." He kissed her cheek. "Now, sweetheart, let's concentrate on your future husband."

She nestled in his arms. "I never thought we'd be together."

At the trading post on the third break of day, the outlaws made plans to leave in separate departures.

Larson and Leech were preparing to leave first with Carol and meet Charlie at the tall red tower rising from the snowy mountain ridge to the west, its highest point easily seen from the post. Leech would wait there for the rest of the gang to join them on a trail that would be marked for them.

While Carol waited in her room at the post, they saddled fresh horses. Larson's trail-weary pinto would be left behind. They had packed a mule with her new belongings.

The two Longley brothers, along with Target and Turner, were required to remain at the station. They were charged with making sure no witnesses were left alive, but to lie about it to Carol when they joined up, letting her believe no one was killed.

At the barn, with Carol still in the main house, Thatch, Leech, and the Longley brothers stood with Larson and spoke in low voices.

Larson addressed the Longleys. "Thatch will be with me and my lady, and we'll be riding on ahead. Charlie will leave a marked trail. And Leech will be waiting for you at the red rock, but I need you to stay here two more nights before you do any killing."

Buck Longley reacted with suspicion. "Why?"

"We don't know if Charlie will have found a pass, and if we have to turn back, I don't want my lady to see the old people dead."

"Yeah, sure," Buck agreed, thinking of all the liquor, food, and comfort at the post.

"Not likely anyone else will happen along, but deal with them the same way. Just don't leave any witnesses. And be sure to turn all the animals loose when you leave."

Buck Longley nodded. "But what about Target and Turner? They're useless."

"I need them to throw to the wolves," Larson said, reflecting. "But I figure if you haven't seen a posse or anyone else by the time you leave, we're in the clear."

"And?"

"So, the two of you," he said to the brothers, "come back alone."

As the satisfied brothers left, Thatch made a face. "Those two give me the creeps."

"We need 'em for awhile longer."

"I sure hope they do let the animals out."

Both Larson and Thatch were animal lovers, and yet had no regrets in killing any man who got in their way. Larson respected women more than Thatch, who saw them as a convenience for his own appetite, but Larson had no choice when it came to leaving any witnesses, including the elderly Mrs. Grossman.

Larson added more. "It's better Charlie don't know what's happening to the old couple, so when you catch up with us, just let him and my lady think they were left alive."

"Why? What would he do?"

"Probably disappear on us," Larson said.

Thatch adjusted the cinch on his saddle. "I can make that happen, anytime you say."

"Without him, we'd be lost in the mountains. We need him to get back to the hideout."

"You think your cousins are already there with the loot?"

Larson turned his back to hide his hate for this greedy man. "Yeah."

"Save the Indian for me. I've waited all this time to blow his brains out."

"You don't have to be so colorful," Larson said, "and not around my lady."

"Yeah. You're sure lucky. She's right beautiful."

Larson didn't like a brutal killer even commenting on his beloved, but he didn't want to raise any trouble until they were close to the hideout.

Leech came over to them and was looking strained. "I don't like the idea of sitting up there by that rock for two nights and then having to ride with them Longleys. Why don't we just head out and leave them holding the bag?"

"Because they got big mouths," Larson said. "But they want their share, so they won't make any trouble if we bring 'em along."

"Yeah, well, I think I should get a bonus for this job," Leech argued.

"You will," Larson promised but thought, *Your bonus will be the same one they're going to get. Six feet under.*

CHAPTER SIX

For another two nights, after Larson left with Carol, Thatch, and Leech to meet Charlie at the red rock, the elderly couple and the two hands at the post were watched like hawks by the Longley brothers. Turner and Target, however, were becoming pets of Mrs. Grossman.

While she was cooking a ham, Turner was playing a jig on his mouth harp, and Target, his belly bouncing, danced around like he had bugs in his britches.

The Longley brothers, disgusted, would head outside to the barn, perhaps feeling the first touch of guilt over what they had to do with the elderly couple.

Early morning of the third day, after chores and breakfast, the Grossmans and the two hands were locked in the storm cellar, which had a ground-level trapdoor near the back porch. Target and Turner made sure they were comfortable with blankets, food and water, and lanterns, leaving the prisoners unaware that they would be murdered by mid-afternoon.

When Target wrapped a blanket around Mrs. Grossman in the lamplight, she smiled at him and Turner. "You boys don't belong with those other men. Why don't you stay with us?"

Target flushed with pleasure but just shrugged. He and Turner left the cellar and stood aside as Buck Longley latched down the door.

Turner and Target had no idea they were about to be murdered as well. They only wondered if there was some way to save the Grossmans. They went inside to find liquor and cookies to take to the front porch.

At the same time, Buck and Sid headed for the barn to saddle up.

"Going to rain," Buck said, glancing at the darkening sky and the clouds moving in from the north.

"Maybe it'll cover our tracks."

"I'll finish here. Go see what we might have missed in the house."

"Then what?" Sid asked.

"Then we'll wipe out the basement and those two clowns."

"Leech better be waiting for us."

"He always does what Larson tells him."

"What does Larson tell him when we're not around?" Sid grunted.

"Just think of all that gold waiting for us."

Both brothers had their doubts about Larson's promises, but they also had no qualms about finishing Larson off the same as anyone else.

After raiding the supply of whiskey, Target and Turner settled on the front porch, which had a high roof. Eating cookies and drinking was how they rewarded themselves and how they escaped reality.

They were unaware that Sid Longley was back in the house, stealing what more he could. Or that Buck waited with the horses at the barn. Or that they were on the murder list. Instead, they sat in chairs with their boots up on the porch railing, hoping the whiskey would keep them from thinking about what they had been ordered to do.

Looking across from the post, above the creek to the west, they could see that the high terrain was formidable. They considered how the creek road ran north and south. From the east, the wagon road ended at the post. Escape was more and more a thought, but they were afraid they couldn't get away from the Longleys. They would have to ride it out and hope Larson kept his promises about the gold.

"Can't let this go to waste," Turner said, tossing an empty bottle and reaching for more.

"We'll be pie-eyed if we don't stop," Target replied with a brief chuckle.

They gazed at the distant red landmark barely visible in the high mountain pass. They had been told that Leech was to wait for them at the bottom of that red spire. They now stared north, up at the cliff, and the dark clouds headed their way.

Target burped and leaned back further. "We catch up with Larson and we get to his hideout, you trust him to share in his cache?"

"No, but what choice do we have?"

"Stay behind?"

"They'd never let us stay here alive."

Drinking had not erased their troubles and they were rattled once more.

Target made a face. "One thing I know, we can't let the Longleys kill these nice folks. Especially the lady."

"Yeah, she reminds me of my old granny."

"And she gave me extra bacon," Target added. "I ain't had that since I ran away from home as a kid."

"Me neither. So how do we stop it?" Turner asked.

"Thing is, we did a lot of bragging to join the escape and share in the loot, but I ain't never killed anyone, no how."

Target grinned briefly. "Me neither."

"So now what?"

"Well," Turner said, "we can't take the Longleys. Not face-on."

"You got any ideas?"

"No."

Both were silent for a time, wondering if they had the guts to back-shoot two men. Anything less and they themselves would be dead.

Abruptly, Target sat up and squinted to the north. "I just saw some riders high on the ridge."

"Where?" Turner saw everything fuzzy for a moment.

Target leaned forward, picked up his rifle. "Right behind that big boulder that's split on top. See? About halfway up."

"You think it's a posse?"

"No, they got a woman with 'em," Target said, working a shell into the chamber of his repeater.

Turner dropped his boots to the deck. "If we don't warn 'em, the Longleys will kill 'em, for sure."

"Yeah, let's scare 'em away. Maybe that'll make the Longleys take off, so they don't have time to kill these nice folks."

Halfway down the rise overlooking the post from the north, with a good view of the front porch, the small posse reined up and took cover in the boulders and brush. They had kept to the high ground above the wagon road to avoid ambush. Now they had come as far down as they could before being exposed.

They felt the damp air that predicted those fast-moving clouds were going to drop buckets of rain within the hour.

Through several narrow openings, they could see the front of the house, and had clear shots to the porch where two men lounged. The corrals out back were visible but only part of the barn could be seen.

"We don't know who they are," Finnegan worried as Bonnie squirmed in front of him on the saddle.

Kansas turned to Billy and Leslie. "You two cover us from up here. If they start shooting, pin 'em down."

"Yeah," Billy said. "But what if they don't miss?"

"We'll take that chance," Finnegan said.

"Billy can stay," Leslie said, perturbed. "I'm going with you."

"You're staying here," Kansas told her.

"Who made you the big he-bull?" she snapped.

She and Kansas glared at each other.

Finnegan intervened. "Miss Leslie, we need a sharp-shooter up here, to protect us."

She gave Kansas a snippy look and finally nodded. As she stepped down from the saddle, Finnegan handed her Bonnie. Kansas gave Billy the lead to the pack horse.

Leslie set the squirming Bonnie on the ground.

Holding his rifle, Billy dismounted to move their mounts and the pack horse safely to the rear. Then he joined Leslie behind the split-top boulder and moved to watch through one of many openings through the rocks. Looking down at the front porch, they watched the two men with their boots on the rail.

They could see horses standing in the corral behind the post building.

"Wait," Leslie said all of a sudden. "That's Larson's pinto in the corral."

"That means you could be riding into an ambush," Billy warned Kansas and Finnegan.

"Just stay put," Kansas said, turning his horse to take the lead.

"You are mule-headed!" Leslie called to Kansas, who ignored her.

As the two riders headed down the steep trail, Billy looked at Leslie.

"Are you mad at Kansas?"

Leslie had a silly smile. "No, I just don't like being bossed."

"Yeah, he tries to boss me around, too, but I just laugh it off."

Billy grinned briefly, then peered through the opening at the post far below.

Leslie found a spot to see clearly, but her mind was on Kansas. *Finally*, she mused, *a man I can take face-on. And maybe hog-tie before he gets away.*

Bonnie ran around, fidgeting as if she knew there was going to be trouble.

Finnegan and Kansas rode down the narrow path toward the flat below. Their horses fought to keep steady on rocks and slippery mud while avoiding scrub junipers and protruding rock formations.

It had already begun to sprinkle.

On the porch, Target and Turner leaned forward from their chairs, rifles resting on the rail. They had spotted Kansas and Finnegan on their way down.

"Try not to hit 'em," Target mumbled.

When they started firing all around the two riders on the down grade, their targets took cover in the rocks and brush. It was obvious the men on the porch never intended to hit anyone.

"Keep 'em back," Turner urged as they kept firing.

At that moment, rifle fire exploded from the area of the split-top boulder high above the riders. Billy's warning shots mainly hit the base of the porch and the front of the house.

Bonnie ran around in circles behind Leslie and barked.

Leslie's shots peppered the rail, spinning Target's bottle off of it, and kept up a barrage that had the two men dropping to their hands and knees and trying to crawl to the front door. With the door hit again and again, the two lay frozen facedown on the deck.

Inside the house, rattled by the shots, Sid Longley peered out from behind the front window's curtains. Seeing the two outlaws flat on the porch deck and not moving, he thought they were dead. He turned from the window and sped to the back door. He met Buck halfway to the barn.

"It's a posse!" Sid blurted. "Sounds like a dozen of 'em."

From where they stood, they could not see past the house to the riders.

Buck made a face. "We can't leave those two clowns to talk."

"They're dead. Lets' go!"

Buck hesitated. "What about the prisoners?"

"If we take time to kill 'em, we'll be caught and hanged, " Sid told him.

"You're right."

"Besides, they was told we were riding south with the creek road."

"Then we can't let 'em see us cross the creek. Head for the trees."

They ran for the saddled horses and the pack mule, jumping on board and riding out of sight behind the barn, across the wide creek and into the trees beyond, where they hoped to be out of sight. On their way to the red rock, they never looked back, just happy to escape what they thought was one heck of a big posse as the barrage continued.

* *

Back on the front porch under continued gunfire, Target and Turner were afraid to move and remained facedown on the deck. Now the shots were spaced out just often enough to keep them prone and helpless.

Rain then burst from the darkening sky, battering the post and porch roof.

It wasn't long before Kansas and Finnegan rode up to the railing and dismounted with rain pouring off their hats, at which point the rifle fire from the ridge came to a halt.

When Kansas stepped onto the porch, he looked down at Target and Turner, still sprawled facedown. He kicked their rifles aside. Rain splattered all around and an icy wind had risen, throwing the wet at them.

"Don't shoot," Turner gasped.

As the men were allowed to sit up, both prisoners caught sight of Finnegan's badge.

"Geez," Target muttered.

Finnegan covered Kansas as he collected their revolvers and allowed the prisoners to get on their knees.

"On your feet," Kansas ordered, backing away as the men stood. "Where's Larson?"

"Gone. Three days ago," Target said.

"Where are the Grossmans?" Finnegan demanded.

"In the cellar," Target said. "With their two hands. But they're all okay."

"Yeah," Turner said, "but it's a good thing you got here. They was gonna be killed by the Longley brothers."

"And where are they?"

"They must have left when the shooting started," Turner speculated, nodding west. "Headed for that red rock. One of 'em is waiting for us there."

Through the heavy rain, the posse could only glimpse the red spire. As Finnegan signaled to Leslie and Billy, Kansas herded the prisoners inside.

While the posse came together at the post, and the prisoners in the storm cellar were being freed, the Longley brothers continued making their way in the driving rain, riding uphill through shrubs and pines, aiming at the often-spotted red spire. The graveled but muddied earth and jagged rocks were hard on the horses. The brothers wore slickers but their britches were wet and their hat brims sagged.

By now, they were so into the heavy, wooded terrain, they could no longer see the post or the creek.

"Them old folks could do a lot of talking," Buck complained.

"They think we're following the creek south."

"Yeah, I know, but they can still describe us."

Sid nodded. "But we didn't kill anybody there, so even if the posse gets real smart and comes this way, we'll just make a deal and sic 'em on Larson."

"Yeah, but they ain't gonna. No one would figure we would try to cross these mountains. It's straight up. And the peaks are covered with snow."

Hunkering down in the rain as it poured off their hat brims, Buck growled at the discomfort. "We sure won't be leaving any tracks in these rocks, but no use getting Leech riled up. As far as he's gonna know, there ain't no posse."

"You're right. He can just figure we did our job."

"I sure hope he has some hot coffee."

Buck swayed in the saddle as his horse slid in the mud, then regained its footing. "All I want is what Larson promised. Enough of a share to live high and mighty."

"You trust 'im?" Buck asked.

"No, but if the gold is there, nobody's gonna stop us from getting it."

While the Longleys headed up the grade to join Leech at the red rock, all was quiet back at the post. The two prisoners, Target and Turner, were hobbled and allowed near the stove to keep warm.

The posse heard from the Grossmans that the outlaws had planned to go south along the creek, but that story was corrected by the two prisoners, who talked again about the red-rock spire. All the while, Mrs. Grossman was feeding them and fussing over them like a grandmother.

Out on the front porch with coffee in hand, watching the rain lighten up, Finnegan, Grossman, and Kansas sat on chairs.

"You can see the red spire from here when it's not raining," Grossman told them. "But no one can cross those mountains. Least, not anyone who went up there was ever heard from again. It's just not passable."

"I crossed over it, once," Finnegan said. "Maybe ten years ago. Prospecting."

"Then you were lucky," the trader said.

"It was a one-way trip," Finnegan admitted. "I came back a different way, below the border. My mother didn't raise any foolish sons."

"You know," Grossman said as he downed his coffee, "my wife is real fond of those two fellahs inside. She's kind of adopted them. And I don't figure they've ever shot anyone in their lives."

"They do seem kind of useless," Finnegan said. "I wonder why Larson kept 'em along with him."

"Throw-aways," Kansas said.

Grossman shrugged. "If you're hungry, my wife's got some biscuits and beans about ready."

Finnegan took another look at the top of the red rock barely visible in the west, then he and Kansas followed the trader back inside.

All enjoyed a hot meal. Then the two hands went back to the barn where they had a bunkhouse with their own stove, and a chance to catch up on their sleep. Billy and Finnegan had followed them out earlier to make sure all was clear and safe.

Mrs. Grossman kept dishing out extras until everyone was stuffed. Leslie assisted in clearing the table and refilled the coffee cups before sitting down.

The prisoners, seated now back near the wall and close to the stove, looked half asleep, but kept waking up as their hostess shoved cookies at them. Mr. Grossman yawned and retreated to a seat by the warm stove.

Kansas took his coffee out on the porch to have a look around.

Leslie, Finnegan, and Billy were feeling weary. After the hot meal, the sound of rain and wind made them all the more sleepy.

"Sure is wet out there," Billy said.

Bonnie went over to the prisoners and ran around their feet. Then she jumped onto Target's lap. "Hey, little girl, what's your name?"

"That's Bonnie," Billy said from over at the table. "She don't like nobody."

At that point, Bonnie jumped up higher and was on Target's chest, licking his face so much, he laughed. He set her down on the floor, and then she had to do the same to Turner.

"I guess you boys must be okay," Mrs. Grossman said. "That puppy likes you."

Turner took out his mouth harp with Bonnie on his lap and played a lively tune. Bonnie barked at him, jumped off, and headed back to Finnegan. Turner laughed and stopped playing.

The tune had awakened Grossman, who accepted a fresh cup of coffee from his wife.

Kansas, who had been out checking the perimeter, returned for more coffee.

Finnegan took charge of Bonnie, holding her on his lap.

Mrs. Grossman chided the two prisoners. "You both need to change your ways."

"Yeah, but look at us. We ain't going nowhere," Turner said.

"Sheriff," she said to Finnegan, "if you parole these big oafs to us, we'll grub-stake them and send them off to the mines up north."

Target and Turner had big, anxious grins.

Finnegan pretended a sour face. Kansas also looked overly grim. Both were putting on a show for the prisoners.

Billy, on the other hand, looked happy about the offer.

Leslie recounted her experience in Larson's camp. "These two helped me and my friend Marianne. They made sure we had enough to eat. They gave us extra food and blankets."

Mrs. Grossman persisted. "We'll be responsible."

Kansas and Finnegan looked at Mr. Grossman, who shrugged and nodded.

"My wife is usually right. When we were locked in the cellar, these two went out of their way to bring us blankets, food and water."

Mrs. Grossman persisted further. "Well, sheriff?"

Finnegan, looking grim, chose to drag it out a bit longer and questioned the prisoners. "Are you worth it?

Turner and Target sputtered their agreement.

"We never did kill nobody," Turner said. "We went to prison on account of we tried to rustle some cattle and got caught before we could move 'em out."

"So," Finnegan said sternly. "You are inept?"

"What's that mean?" Target asked, looking strained.

"You can't do anything right," Finnegan said.

"Wait," Kansas said to the prisoners, "how far did you move the cattle? Across their property line?"

"Heck, no," Turner said, "they was so wild, they kept dodging us and running away."

"So," Kansas said, "you were just trespassing, Ten days in jail, not prison."

"All we know is, the cattle belonged to some rich dude who got real mad," Target said, "and we got sent up."

"So why were you with Larson?" Leslie demanded.

"Hey, they were breaking out and invited us along," Turner said. "I was getting sick from what they was feeding us in there. One day I saw bugs in the slop!"

Finnegan kept a straight face and glared at the prisoners. "If these fine folks take custody, are you gonna do right by them? Pay back your grub stake?"

"Yeah," Turner and Target said in unison.

Mrs. Grossman smiled. "They get out of hand, all I have to do is feed them. They're really just big puppy dogs."

Now the whole posse was smiling and chuckling.

Mrs. Grossman walked around to where Finnegan sat and bent over to kiss his cheek. Finnegan had a silly look. Bonnie tried to leap up to lick her face but Finnegan set her on the floor again.

"And," Mrs. Grossman said, turning to the prisoners, "we have to change how you look. Grow beards. And you need baths. Some decent clothes. And change your names. You will be our cousins."

Target and Turner could not believe their good fortune.

"And you, Miss Leslie," Mrs. Grossman said. "We'll have to get you out of those torn clothes. Soon's I can heat some water, we'll fill a tub for you to clean up. And I have just the outfit for you."

Leslie responded with a grateful smile.

"And the two of you are pretty messy," Mrs. Grossman said, giving the nervous Kansas and Finnegan the once over.

Finnegan tried to distract her by telling her and her husband, "We need to leave a letter with you to send along with your next supply wagon. We have to let the sheriff know that Larson is alive."

"Done," Mr. Grossman said. "Might even be faster with the next mule train."

That same afternoon, Kansas went out on the porch once again to survey the area for safety. The wind had subsided and the rain was lighter. He stood by the rail and sipped his coffee. He was only watching the rain for a few minutes before Leslie joined him.

"That was a decent thing you and Mr. Finnegan just did."

"I would have hanged them." He met her stare and almost smiled. "Well, maybe not, and could be they'll make the Grossman's rich if they find the mother lode."

"You're a strange man, Kansas."

He turned his back to look toward the wide creek to their left. She followed his gaze all the way to the red rock now half-shrouded by dark clouds. They noted the rough terrain they'd have to navigate.

She gestured. "It's maybe half a day's ride up there. We should head out while it's still daylight."

"We'll leave late tonight. In time to arrive before daybreak."

"It's still raining and could get worse. It'd be dangerous for the horses in the dark. "

He knew she was right, but they had no choice.

"Why is it you men never listen to me?" she demanded. "Don't you know?"

"Why, because I'm female?"

His back to her to hide his smile, he stood firm. "That's right."

"Why, you… you man, you!"

"You said it well."

She stormed around to face him. "Are you trying to make me angry?"

"Yes."

Their gaze met, and she almost sputtered. "Well, you've succeeded."

"I've never met a beautiful woman who had any sense."

"Flattery doesn't work on me, you know!"

He realized what he'd said and backed off. "I didn't say *you* were beautiful."

He walked to the edge of the porch, his back to her again and his hand on the rail, trying not to laugh.

She glared after him and forced her way in front of him, shoving him back a few steps. "Listen, Kansas Red, I can out-shoot and out-ride you any day."

"That remains to be seen."

Exasperated, she put her hands on her hips. "So why are we waiting until the middle of the night in a rain storm?"

"The red rock looks to be well above the timberline."

"So?"

"Right now, we'd be approaching their camp in daylight with little cover."

Stopped cold, realizing he was right, she reddened.

He returned to the rail to stare toward the red rock in the distance.

"You're right," she said, feeling foolish.

He didn't respond, but his thoughts were busy. *You're a*

sharpshooter. And you are smart. And tough. But you're too darn beautiful for your own good.

Her thoughts were more humorous. *Okay, Kansas Red, so you're dancing around me and playing games. But you are underestimating a Texas woman. When I swing a loop, I don't miss, so watch out.*

Finally, she stood at the rail next to him and followed his gaze west.

"I know Larson is headed for some valley beyond these mountains," she said. "And he has to cross another range beyond that to get to his hideout. He has cousins meeting them there. They're supposed to bring a huge amount of gold, but I don't think Larson intends to share it with his men like he promised."

"What are his plans, beyond that?"

"I heard him telling Carol they would set sail to South America and start a new life, so they have to be headed for California."

"He murdered her husband. Why would she even—"

"They have a history of some kind." Kansas was suddenly so grim, she quickly changed the subject. "Mrs. Grossman has apple pie in the oven. Can you smell it?"

"Yes."

At that moment, Finnegan came outside and pulled a chair back from the railing. He sat as Bonnie, trailing, leaped onto his lap and settled down.

Kansas drew a chair near him, but Leslie remained at the rail at some distance. Now the wind returned and blew rain on her, and she backed away under the porch.

"Mrs. Grossman has a bath ready for you, Miss Leslie," Finnegan said.

Kansas grunted and wrinkled his nose without looking at her. "About time."

She spun and glared down at him, but he would not meet her gaze as she snapped at him. "Speak for yourself, stinky."

As Leslie charged back in the house, Finnegan chuckled. "You're not going to win with that one."

Kansas tried to stay sober, but he had to smile and admit he was getting a kick out of her.

"We're next for a bath," Finnegan added with a grin. "I'll bet Mrs. Grossman wants to scrub us clean."

"That'll be the day."

"But the girl's right, you know. We could be fighting the rain all night."

Kansas nodded, reluctant to admit she was right. "We have no choice."

The two men were silent a long while, then Kansas gestured. "So you've been beyond that red cliff?"

"Just that once. It's rough going for a lot of days before you hit a small valley. It's named Donovan's Flats after his general store on the north-south wagon road. First off, there's an old mission, but most of the Utes have moved north. Father John was running it, if he's still there."

"Right on Larson's trail."

"I know what you're thinking, but nobody would kill a priest."

"Larson would."

"Let's pray not," Finnegan scowled.

Inside, Leslie was back in a private room where, behind a silver screen, she enjoyed a hot bath in an iron tub. She washed off days of grime, which left her feeling soft and feminine. She washed her hair, which turned from dirty blonde to flaxen gold once more. She let Mrs. Grossman outfit her with blue riding skirts actually designed for side-saddle but full enough to be comfortable on a man's saddle. It came with a white blouse and a blue jacket. A new wide-brimmed hat with chin strap came with the outfit.

Mrs. Grossman also provided a heavy coat. "Gets cold in those mountains," she said. "We'll make sure all of you have enough blankets and a tarp."

"You're very generous," Leslie said, admiring herself in the mirror.

"We owe our lives to all of you," Mrs. Grossman said. "Now tell me about your man, that Kansas."

"He's not my man."

"I heard you on the porch. You've got him on the run."

Leslie flashed a smile. "He's going to be really hard to catch."

"Be careful, child. You don't know if those dime novels are true. He could be a really bad man. A killer."

"No one is as bad as Larson."

"That doesn't say much." Mrs. Grossman handed her a scarf.

Leslie nodded. "But when they found me half-dead on the trail, it was Kansas who held my hand and let me cling to his side the whole night long."

"Oh, my."

They walked back into the front room where Mr. Grossman was making fresh coffee at the stove. No one else was in the room.

"Where are your new prospectors?" Leslie asked, referring to Target and Turner.

"They went out to help clean the barn."

"They also need a bath," Leslie said.

The trader nodded. "I figured they might as well get good and dirty first."

Mrs. Grossman giggled. "It's going to be a lot of fun."

*　　*　　*　　*

While the post was conducting bath-time that same night, the Longley brothers were still fighting the steep terrain. At first light, they spotted a campfire under a rock overhang by the red cliff. It was above the timber line and open but rocky.

They rode up to the camp where Leech was wrapped in blankets and fighting to keep the fire going. Wind and rain sometimes swept under the rock cover. They dismounted and left their horses where Leech had his next to a boulder, which broke some of the wind. They hurried to kneel by the fire and reach for coffee and beans.

"What took you so long?" Leech grumbled.

"It was not an easy job," Buck lied, shivering as he downed some coffee.

"All dead?" Leech asked.

"Yeah, that's right." Buck reached for a plate of beans.

"We got a long way to go to catch up," Leech said. "They'll be waiting at the mission."

"How are we going to get there?" Sid wanted to know as he sipped his coffee. "We get deep into these mountains, we could get lost."

"It's due west," Leech said, wishing he could leave them behind. "But Charlie's going to mark trees or leave rock signs to keep us going."

"They're still three days ahead of us," Buck complained.

"Yes, but we'll head out soon as your horses can make it."

"You been with Larson a lot of years," Sid said to Leech. "He keep his word?"

"Always."

Buck downed his beans. "He said we'll get a share of the gold dust he took from the post. And some real gold when we get to the hideout. Think it's true?"

"Yeah," Leech said, believing it because Larson had indeed

always been truthful with his men. He was unaware that was about to change.

None of them knew Larson would be wiping out anyone who would otherwise be left behind and could say he was still alive.

They would ride another full day before the signs started to disappear.

*   *   *   *

High in the mountains where the peaks often blocked the view of all but a little sky, and three days ahead of Leech and the Longleys, Larson camped in a half-cave in the face of a gnarled cliff. Carol was still asleep further back in the hollow as daylight came.

It was still raining but the wind had died down.

Thatch and Larson were over by the fire. Charlie had gone down to the horses in the trees to check on them, except the Ute had circled back around the rocks and stopped within earshot, while unseen.

"Well," Larson said in a low voice. "So far, so good."

Thatch murmured. "But how long are we going to leave a trail?"

"One more day. I'll relieve Charlie of that job and send him on ahead, because I want to leave signs that will point north into the peaks where they'll get lost for good. The rain will hide which way we headed."

Larson didn't mind losing Leech in order to be rid of the Longleys, who were not only fearsome but, to Larson, capable of turning on their leader if they saw a chance.

"You think Charlie knows we left everyone dead at the post?"

"No. Neither does my lady, and I don't want either one of them to ever know."

After pouring himself more coffee, Thatch thought ahead. "You're sure that mission is on our way?"

"I remember it from when my uncle and I trailed south along Donovan's Creek, maybe three years ago, so it should still be there. And there's a general store, so we can load up on coffee and supplies."

"But you still need the Indian?"

"Yeah, there's still another mountain range to cross. If he can find a pass."

"Well, the way we been fighting these rocky cliffs, I don't know if you can call this a pass."

Larson sipped his coffee. "The rougher the better, so we won't have anyone on our tail."

Charlie had heard everything, and figured he would stay for the second mountain range so that Carol would survive. But before leaving, he would help himself to some gold dust one night and then just disappear, but only once he knew Carol would be safe.

That same night, the posse left the trading post in the rain.

CHAPTER SEVEN

Four days after Larson had left the post, and just before dawn, the posse used the cover of rain and lingering darkness to approach the open space between the pines and the red spire.

Kansas, Billy, Leslie, and Finnegan, with Bonnie on his saddle and tucked under his slicker, were ready for anything with their rifles primed. Cold gusts of wind iced their faces and bare hands in first light.

They saw no signs of life as they approached the camp which was sheltered by a rock overhang. Kansas rode on ahead but found it abandoned and signaled the others to follow.

They took time for a campfire and breakfast out of the rain, with plans to sleep awhile. Their horses were also spent, and they knew they had to take it slow.

"Won't be easy tracking them," Finnegan said.

Billy downed his coffee. "I thought you were a tracker."

"Mostly by instinct," Finnegan replied. "How about you, Kansas?"

"The same," Kansas replied. "But most often there's a sign like a loose horse shoe or a rock out of place."

"What about you?" Billy asked Leslie.

She shook her head.

"She may not be a tracker," Finnegan said, "but she can witch for water."

"Yeah," Billy said. "I seen her do it on the Walker ranch. With a stick."

"Did you say witch?" Kansas persisted, checking his revolver, pretending to be sour.

She made a face at him and thought, *I don't need to be a witch to put a spell on you, Kansas Red.*

After some sleep, they were back on the trail. Riding over rocks and through brush, they soon discovered several rock piles left in the shape of arrows to guide the outlaws had been poorly scattered.

*   *   *   *

Some three days ahead of the posse, Larson, Thatch, Carol, and Charlie rode onto the rise overlooking an almost treeless valley under a partly cloudy sky. Green and glistening from the rain, it spread a few miles west and then north and south with farms and ranches scattered across. They could see the north-south wagon road, near which stood the general store. Behind the building, a fast-moving creek sped over rocks and around brush.

Beyond to the west, a formidable wall of snow-crested cliffs awaited them.

Cattle grazed across the grassland. A row of fruit trees with white blossoms stood near a farmhouse.

And closer, down below on their side of the flats, they saw the mission, red of adobe and rocks, off by itself with a cemetery, and huts that had housed many of the Utes before they moved north. A few cottonwoods stood along the nearby creek. Goats were in a corral by themselves, horses grazing near the trees.

Leech, Thatch and Charlie headed down the steep trail.

Larson and Carol remained a moment longer at the top of the rise, and he reached out to take her hand. "This is it, honey," he said.

"Are you sure it's safe to use your real name?"

"I want it to be legal on paper."

She beamed with love. "Thank you."

"When we get to California, we'll use another name with the sailing ship, but you'll always have proof you're a respectable married lady. When we find our new home in South America, we'll be the Larsons again."

"I'm so glad."

"Besides, my name means nothing here." He gestured west beyond the valley to the next rise of imposing mountains. "One more crossing."

"That's the only way?"

"I know it's been hard, sweetheart, but it's safer, and only a fool would try to follow us. And we have Charlie."

"Could we stop at the store?"

"Anything you like," he said, leading the way downhill. "But first things first."

At the mission, there was smoke curling from the chimney. Out back, an elderly Ute Indian tended graves, pulling weeds. He stood up, wiped his brow.

Larson and his party dismounted in front of the mission and entered where they were greeted by Father John, a friendly pious man who was happy to conduct a wedding.

The room was cluttered with benches and donated furniture and goods. The bride and groom removed their coats for the ceremony.

Carol wore a new gingham dress. The lace she had taken from

Grossman's served as a veil, which fell from her flaxen hair and reached to the floor. Charlie and Thatch stood as their witnesses.

When Father John pronounced them man and wife, Larson kissed his willing bride, who was tearful but smiling.

Out of caution and by instinct in studying the dangerous Thatch, the priest only wrote their names on the certificate he presented to the happy couple. He would make his own record later.

Larson saw no signs of a registry and assumed the priest had no reason to keep a record. As they left the building, he also saw distant wagons with families arriving for a church service, and made a hasty withdrawal before they arrived.

*　　*　　*　　*

Meanwhile, the posse continued on what appeared to be a deer trail with occasional hoof prints. The morning brought a partly cloudy sky with occasional sprinkles turning to rain. To the west, snow-covered peaks rose all the more in their path.

The posse, deep in heavy terrain, was able to find tracks, and when they could not, they let Bonnie sniff along ahead of them.

Bonnie was often distracted by critters in the brush and got tangled in briars more than once. Worried about her, Finnegan finally put her back on the saddle in front of him. Cliffs and boulders often closed in on them, tricking their instincts.

A half day ahead of them under a cloudy sky, Leech and the Longleys had been following arrows formed by little rocks, which they'd been scattering along the way, but the signs had stopped the night before. Not even a chip mark on a tree.

"What the devil?" Buck snarled, on foot and leading his horse. "They cut us off."

"Maybe we took a wrong turn," Leech replied, hopeful.

"If you ask me," Sid growled, "they want us to get lost up here."

"Larson would never do that," Leech said, but now he was worried.

They were muttering over it when snow began to fall, fluttering down around them.

"Wait," Sid growled, pointing northward to a new but single arrow of stones. "They're heading north for some reason."

"No," Leech said, "it's a trick to lose us for good up here. We'll keep going west."

"I thought you trusted Larson," Buck said.

Leech shook his head. "Not anymore."

They were deep in snow-dusted cliffs and had to move through thick stands of timber. Only the occasional sun gave them any idea which direction to go. The terrain forced them in other directions, time and again. The elevation took their breath away.

And light snow was falling to further confuse their location.

Now they had to camp, for the horses were worn. They found shelter in a rise of boulders and set up a tarp for a fire.

*   *   *   *

The posse continued west in a dusting of snow. Wary of ambush, they were in no hurry. Kansas led the way.

All of a sudden, Bonnie started barking and squirming.

High on a cliff ahead and to their far right, a mountain lion was moving along the skyline. Bonnie continued to bark as if she was ready to attack it. Ignoring them, the lion disappeared over the ridge. Bonnie whined at her loss.

Later, they saw movement in the grass near some tree trunks. Before long, they spotted two black bear cubs trotting across the trail far ahead and then disappearing into the thick brush.

Finnegan put his hand over Bonnie's mouth to prevent her barking this time.

Trailing the cubs, the sow appeared on the trail and stopped to look at them. Bonnie went wild, squirming and trying to bark despite Finnegan keeping her mouth closed. She was desperate to chase that bear.

Finnegan shoved her under his coat, holding her so she could still breathe but not see the sow. They sat their saddles as quietly as possible. Kansas, in the lead, worked a shell into his repeater's chamber, yet knowing that if the bear decided to charge, his horse might rear and his shot could go wild.

They all sat quiet, waiting.

Wanting to catch up with her frisky cubs, and having no interest in horses, the sow turned and, with flat-footed steps, disappeared into the high brush and trees. They waited until they could see it moving along the grade high above, heading in another direction on the trail of her young.

When the bear was no longer in sight, Finnegan brought Bonnie back to his lap. The little dog no longer saw a target and was exhausted now by the excitement.

Billy grunted to Leslie. "She thinks she's big as they are."

"I want her on my side," Leslie said, amused.

Clouds were soon moving overhead. The air was damp.

Kansas again rode off on a scout, out of sight into the timber and red rock formations, headed north away from the trail.

It was late in the afternoon when the three outlaws, high up on rough terrain, discovered they were being followed. They dismounted behind a rocky formation.

"See?" Buck gestured down through the pines along a narrow path below. "A man on a white mule. I saw a flash of a badge under his coat. They're headed this way. Single file. Can't see how many."

"Let's get the horses down that back slope," Leech said, looking to his right and over his shoulder. "I'll get over where that big pine sits by itself. You two can spread out here."

"Wait till we see 'em all," Buck warned.

Buck made his way north of the trail and got down in the rocks and brush. Sid moved south into the scrub pines.

Leech ended up high enough to their right to see the oncoming riders. He was also in a spot where he could drop down to the horses and high-tail it out while the others tried the ambush.

Now the outlaws could see Finnegan in front, and then Billy, but they were unaware of Leslie, who was trailing and still out of sight. They also had no idea Kansas was coming on to them from their left.

Finnegan, in the lead, had his coat open to show the badge on his vest. He was still in the trees but within easy range when Bonnie started squirming on his lap. Suddenly, she began a deep growl, a warning, without stopping.

"Ambush!" Finnegan shouted. "Take cover!"

The outlaws opened fire with their rifles, missing their targets.

Finnegan and Billy moved deep into the trees on the east side of the trail. Up in the rocks, Kansas was getting in position.

Leslie, further back, moved to the west and dismounted in the boulders before taking cover.

The two outlaw brothers continued firing

"This could go on all day," Buck growled.

"They can't see us," Sid replied. "Take our time, and we'll get 'em all."

"Where's Leech?"

Buck gestured to their right. "I saw him moving around the hill to get a better shot."

"Yeah, where the horses are."

Buck glowered. "He'd better not be taking off."

They could not see that Leech had already made it to the horses further down behind the ambush site.

Leslie, however, had moved fast and now, high in the rocks, could see Leech as he spotted her, spun his horse, and fired.

Leslie's rifle barked. Leech jerked, yanked on the reins as he died, and was thrown into the rocks with a crushing thud.

"Sounds like he didn't make it," Sid muttered from where he crouched. They still could not see Leslie.

"Yeah, and now we're surrounded," Buck snapped.

The brothers fired rapidly at where they thought the posse was shooting from, but they didn't see Kansas rising above them.

"Up with your hands," Kansas shouted down at them.

They spun and fired upward, but Kansas returned fire at the same time.

The brothers were both hit and collapsed where they crouched, Buck firing one last shot into the ground.

All three outlaws were now dead.

Later that day, the posse completed the burials. They unsaddled the outlaws' horses and brought them into camp as the night had turned so cold, blankets were not enough. They hurriedly gathered brush and chips. Sheltered under a rock overhang, they built a fire as it began to snow again.

Bonnie, their heroine, received a great deal of attention.

They all huddled close to the struggling fire and tried to come up with a plan.

"We're not going anywhere soon," Finnegan said.

"We'll lose the trail markings," Billy complained.

"We already have," Kansas said. "It seems intentional."

"So they wanted to lose them up here?" Billy questioned.

"Yes," Kansas said. "But the trail so far has been due-west, so we'll just follow the sun."

"When we can see it," Billy whispered to himself.

Kansas stared into the fire, not letting them see he was worried.

"But," Leslie popped up, "Mr. Finnegan has already crossed these mountains, right?"

Finnegan nodded. "Maybe I'll remember as we go along."

Surrounded by high peaks, they knew they could just as easily be lost forever.

Yet, days later, when they came to a wall of cliffs, Finnegan remembered he had gone south until he heard the roar of a waterfall. He led them down a narrow deer trail through rocks and brush until they came to the roaring creek.

Finnegan remembered where they could ford, further south, and they were soon on their way west again, but also back in high, rough terrain.

When the posse came to the green valley, they were a full week behind Larson. They could see the mountain range beyond to the west with more steep terrain but not as formidable nor as heavy with snow.

It was windy and cold under a cloudy sky when they rode down the steep grade to the valley floor and on to the mission which was the closest spot.

Billy, Kansas, Leslie, and Finnegan with Bonnie on his saddle reined up at the mission's front gate. Their faces felt frozen as did their feet inside wet boots.

Out of the mission came Father John to greet them and beckon them inside.

They followed and he bade them welcome. It was toasty warm with a fire in the hearth in the front room, with the chapel visible at the rear of the building.

Offered hot coffee, the posse removed their heavy coats and settled down in chairs facing the crackling fire, except for Kansas, who remained standing.

Finnegan, Bonnie in his lap, leaned forward, cup in hand. "Father, we're looking for three or four men, traveling west with a woman. Her name is Carol."

Father John moved near the hearth. "Yes, they were here for a wedding, over a week ago."

Billy gasped, choking on his coffee, his eyes showing great anxiety. His hands were trembling so badly he could hardly hold his cup.

"You keep a record of those you marry?" Kansas asked.

"Yes, I do."

"Were they aware of it?"

"No, they were in a hurry, so I just married them. After they left, I entered the record in my log."

"That saved your life," Kansas said.

"I had that feeling." The priest stood up and went behind a counter to lift up the log book. "It was the last wedding I held."

"And the names?" Kansas persisted.

Billy could hardly breathe as he waited. The priest set the book on the counter and seemed to take forever but finally found the page, reading aloud.

"Carol Cassidy and Thorn Larson."

Billy half rose from his chair. "She was forced! Couldn't you see that?"

"I'm sorry, son," Father John said, closing the log. "But she looked happy, and she said yes. They embraced and…"

"No," Billy sputtered, sinking back in his chair.

Kansas stood silent, staring into the hearth at the flickering red flames.

Leslie reached over to grip Billy's arm, then withdrew.

"Where did they go from here?" Finnegan asked.

"They stopped at the store, but Mr. Donovan said they intended to cross the mountains to the west. He told them those cliffs were steep and dangerous. He advised them to go south and circle around. "

"Did they?" Finnegan persisted.

"No, he said they crossed the creek and headed west toward the cliffs," Father John said.

Billy, nervous and shaken, slid to the edge of his chair. "We've got to go find them. Now."

"Bad move," Finnegan said. "The horses won't make it now. Maybe tomorrow."

"You're welcome to camp behind the mission," Father John said. "There's feed and water."

"We have three extra horses," Finnegan said. "Only one can still travel. The others are stone-bruised and need to be re-shod at some point soon. If you don't mind, we'll leave those for anyone who might need them."

Father John hesitated with a lot of unspoken questions.

"They've been re-branded so many times," Finnegan said, "there's no telling who rightfully owns them. But they are gentle enough for families. And they could be broke to harness."

"I'll see to it," Father John said, relieved, "so, thank you."

Later that night, camped behind the mission under a full moon spreading light in the starry sky, though it was cool, they found it much warmer than where they had been. Billy was up and down, fretting, pacing. Finnegan sat in his blankets with Bonnie in his lap. Kansas stood nearby, coffee cup in hand, staring off into the night. Leslie, wrapped in her own blankets, could not sleep and finally sat up.

The hot campfire crackled and spit but cast welcome heat.

Finnegan cautioned Billy. "If you don't get some sleep, you'll be falling out of the saddle tomorrow."

"Father John—he said she was willing," Billy whined. "How can she be with Larson right after my pa was murdered?"

"Maybe she's pretending," Finnegan offered. "Just to stay alive. And it could be, she didn't want the priest to be harmed if she resisted."

"Yeah," Billy said, walking in circles and desperately clinging to the thought. "That must be it."

Leslie offered her questionable input with as much sincerity as she could muster. "Your mother wants to survive, so she can see you again. You're all she has left."

Billy kept pacing, keeping everyone awake.

Kansas, his face tight with his own thoughts, downed his coffee.

"Kansas, do you think my mother is okay?" Billy asked, getting no response.

Finnegan looked weary. "Kansas, tell him to get some sleep."

Kansas's voice was deep and grim. "Billy, go to sleep."

Billy hesitated, looked at Kansas's burning eyes, then at the concerned Leslie and annoyed Finnegan. Finally, his own exhaustion took over.

"Everybody keeps telling me what to do," Billy said as he collapsed into his bedding.

Hours later in the night, while Billy was settled and asleep in his blankets by the fire, Leslie sat up from hers. She paused to see Finnegan with his eyes closed and Bonnie on his chest, and she noted Kansas was missing. She got to her feet and looked around in the dark beyond the glow of the fire. She took up a blanket and wrapped it about her shoulders, then left the campsite.

She walked in the bright moonlight and saw Kansas off near the goat pen. He was leaning on the corral fence and looking at the mixed range of the animals, young and old, of many colors, all crowded together and lying asleep.

Kansas didn't move as she came to stand a few feet from him. She put her hands on the top fence board which rose to her shoulder height. Kansas, much taller, leaned on the top board.

Fighting with painful memories, Kansas was silent but explosive. He did not want company, yet there was something about her that eased his pain.

"Billy's hurting," she said.

Kansas nodded as he thought, *He's not alone.*

"I thought I knew her," she continued, of Carol. "But when I saw her with Larson, there was so much more going on. Her ring was missing the first day in camp. I don't know their history, but I can tell you for sure, she was not forced to marry him."

I don't want to hear it, but Kansas could not say this out loud.

"I remember being at her wedding to Sam," Leslie said. "She really was very beautiful. So many of the men there were lovesick for her. You could see it everywhere you turned, but I do know that Larson was not there. He was already in prison at the time."

Kansas didn't answer and stared at the distant mountains to the west, a shadow against the horizon. Yes, it would be treacherous to cross, and yet it was a short cut, which only meant Carol and Larson would soon be on their way and possibly out of reach. It was causing him a great deal of stress which Leslie did not see at first.

"It might be better for Billy if he never saw her again," Leslie said. "It's hard enough now. He keeps saying he has no one anymore. I told him we're all his friends, but he grieves for his father, thinks his mother abandoned him, and says he's all by his lonesome in this world."

Kansas continued to look away in silence.

"You and Mr. Finnegan are both so much older and wiser,"

she said, "but it's you who has been out there on your own. Billy reads the dime novels about your adventures. He might listen to you."

Kansas shook his head to disagree. The life he had led as a soldier, bounty hunter, hired gun and loner would bring little wisdom to the boy.

"But his real hero was Sam," she said.

Kansas remained silent, staring off into the moonlight at the rolling hills.

"Except," she said, painfully, "I know Billy was born two months early. I'm terrified that Larson could be his father. Do you know what that would do to him?"

Leslie didn't know what it was doing to Kansas, who wasn't aware there was even the possibility that Billy could be Larson's son. It was the last straw for him. Any man who had kept such a woman on a pedestal for eighteen years had to have been either a fool or a dreamer. Kansas had run out of excuses for his brother's wife, and was now drowning in shame for what he had once treasured.

For a long while, Leslie herself fought off sadness with a great effort. She had lost her own family so many years ago. She had lost two men who had loved her. Her only friends had been Carol and Marianne. Although tough on the outside, she knew what it felt like to be hurt and alone. Except that now, being near Kansas, she felt a deep affection for him that had no sensible explanation. He was ornery, a mostly silent loner who pretended to have no deep feelings of his own. Yet she yearned to be in his arms.

Kansas swallowed hard, his right hand gripping the fence. "You should get some sleep."

She almost reacted with a snappy comeback, but she saw his wet eyes reflect the moonlight as he stared straight ahead.

117

She felt she was witnessing a terrible pain. Now she had more questions but dared not ask.

"Yes," she said. "But so should you, because we need you, Kansas."

To his surprise, she moved closer to his side and pressed her face to his shoulder. She slid her arm under his and moved her fingers into his hand. He had once been at her side all night when she had been badly hurt and needed consolation. Now she wanted to do the same for him.

Just her touch was enough to start his heart racing. She was trouble—testy, combative, and irritating—but she was also soft and warm and comforting.

Kansas had been a lonely man for most of his life, in part because of a foolish love for the wrong woman. Now he wondered if any woman could ever be trusted.

He bit his lip to stop his eyes from watering all the more. Leslie was close, and he remembered holding her once, a moment still with him. He ached to reach out and take her in his arms, to feel the comfort and warmth she could offer.

She stood at his side for a long while, then felt his hand tighten on hers.

In the quiet night, they heard the single hoot of an owl, followed by a far away bark of a farmer's dog. Whereupon, Bonnie's small, shrill bark echoed from the distant fire.

Losing control, sick of the past and overwhelmed by her presence, Kansas turned to draw Leslie into his arms, her face resting on his chest. She pressed close to him and welcomed his strong embrace.

Her shining, tingling hair brushed against his chin. He moved his fingers through the soft tresses low on her back. It was a long while before he released her. Then he turned his back, and even though she longed to still be in his arms, she understood he needed to be alone now. She could only guess at the reasons.

"Good night," she whispered.

Kansas slowly turned to watch her from where he stood, waiting until she was back at the campfire, kneeling and rolling into her blankets. It would not be easy to forget the way she had felt in his arms, so warm and gentle and yet so much a woman. Never had he expected what he felt for her, and it was unnerving on top of what he had kept inside of him for most of his life.

He felt he had wasted too many years. *How could one man be such a fool?*

After a time, he moved back toward camp and stopped short of it for a better look. He could see that Billy and Finnegan, Bonnie on his shoulder, were both asleep but still he waited. He heard crickets near the creek to his far left and saw a small critter scurrying out of sight beyond it.

Still badly shaken, he had to collect himself before walking over to his own blankets. He knelt not far from Leslie and saw that her eyes were closed.

The full moon was slowly being covered by increasing clouds, leaving only occasional and hazy starlight.

Kansas silently prayed as he lay back and closed his eyes.

He knew that what lay ahead could be devastating for all of them, especially the young boy, if what worried Leslie turned out to be true.

It could also be extremely painful for himself.

CHAPTER EIGHT

Early the next morning around a newly-blazing campfire behind the mission, the posse had a hot breakfast under a partly cloudy sky. They sat around with steaming cups of coffee. They could see an elderly Ute tossing hay to the goats, over the fence, some distance back. Bonnie was at the Indian's heels, barking at the animals, which ignored her until she gave up, returned to camp and found Leslie's lap.

Hazy sunlight came from the east over the mountains they had just survived.

Leslie sipped her coffee and held it aside as Bonnie jumped up to lick her face, then jumped down and headed to where Finnegan sat, crawling into his lap, leaping up to lick his right ear, then back to the ground and over to attack Billy's boots as he stood nearby.

"She wants you to play," Finnegan said.

Billy was hurting too much to respond. He just watched Bonnie until she took off again. This time she headed for Kansas's lap, but Kansas just stood up with his steaming cup and stared off to the west. Bonnie pranced around his boots and then headed back to Finnegan's lap.

To the far west, they could see the cliffs and peaks of the next range, patches of snow visible in the early light. If it truly was a shortcut, that meant they could close in on Carol and Larson a little too soon. Kansas himself did not feel ready for that.

Leslie downed her coffee and tried to look unconcerned as she followed Kansas's gaze.

"What's on the other side of those mountains?" she asked Finnegan.

"I've heard there's a boomtown there called Gold Hollow. It's rumored to be a very dangerous place with the mines playing out. Heard it's more of an outlaw hangout now. But we could go south and around and catch up with Larson on the other side."

"Everyone here can decide that," Kansas said, grimly. "I'm not taking any chances. I'm going to be on his heels, all the way."

Billy nodded. "Me, too. And Mr. Finnegan, he can arrest 'im."

"I'm out of my jurisdiction," Finnegan said of his badge.

"He won't know that," Billy insisted. "And he's only got two men with him now."

Finnegan shrugged and looked at Leslie. "You said he had cousins meeting him at some hide out. He say how many of 'em?"

"I don't know, just that they are supposed to be bringing a lot of gold with them."

"That's why he left those others lost in the mountains," Finnegan said, referring to the three that had died when they ambushed the posse. "He didn't want to share."

"It's time," Kansas said, bending to take up his bedroll and saddle.

Finnegan emptied the coffee pot, kicked dirt on the fire, and gathered their gear into a possible sack. Bonnie ran around, sniffing the ground.

"Can we stop at the store?" Leslie asked. "I'm going to need warmer clothes."

"We'll want to talk to them anyway," Finnegan said with a nod.

They were soon saddling up, just as the priest came out the back door of the mission. He had a sack with fresh bread and cheese, which Finnegan gladly accepted.

"I'll pray for you all to be safe," Father John said.

The posse left a generous donation, then rode west from the mission. They had one spare mount and the pack horse. They crossed the green flats where cattle and sheep grazed in different spots, while fat pigs at a homestead snorted and squealed as they passed, getting Bonnie all excited.

A farmer carrying a milk pail came out of a distant barn and waved. They waved back as Bonnie barked from Finnegan's saddle with her teeth trying to chew the horn.

The sky was cloudy, and the wind was rising.

Ahead, beyond the shadows on the green valley, they could see more clearly the sharp rise of the mountains, far beyond the southbound creek.

They reined up in front of Donovan's weatherbeaten store, where it perched on a rise in front of the busy creek and just west of the north/south wagon road.

Inside, Kansas and Finnegan loaded up on shells. Billy was in charge of getting coffee and canned beans. They also bought two additional tarps. Leslie chose a new wide-brimmed hat with a chin strap, a heavier coat and a woolen scarf. Finnegan and Kansas paid for everything, but Leslie promised to repay them, as had Billy.

Answering Finnegan's questions, the middle-aged, stocky, clean-shaven Bob Donovan nodded. "Sure, they were here. The lady bought some ribbons and lace."

"Which way did they go?" Finnegan asked.

"West to the mountains. I told 'em it was a short cut, all right, but mighty steep going. And I warned 'em they'd be running into trouble at Gold Hollow on the far side. There's a pretty rough bunch running it. I advised them to go south and around, but they just ignored me."

"How did she look?" Billy asked, his expression painful.

"Like a blushing bride," the store owner said. "But she wasn't wearing a ring, so he bought her a gold band I had in that jewelry case. And a necklace. She was mighty pleased."

Billy dropped a sack of coffee on the counter and charged outside.

"What's wrong with the boy?" Donovan asked.

"Something he ate," Finnegan said.

"I didn't finish," the store owner added. "I wanted to say the bride also looked real frail and sickly. They bought some canned soups for her."

"Let's see what you have," Finnegan said. "Anything else canned?"

Donovan offered tin cans of meats, beans, and peaches. He also had a new-fangled can opener that looked more like a hole-punch.

When the travelers went back outside with their purchases, they found Billy bending over nearby bushes, having lost his breakfast.

They waited by their mounts until Billy came to down some water from his canteen. He looked pale and spent as he mounted his horse.

Now they had to ford the busy creek.

*   *   *   *

Still days ahead of the posse, camped before nightfall against a yellow cliff on the far side of the mountains, Larson and Carol shivered beside a struggling fire. They were looking down the final drop to the green valley spread beyond with rolling hills.

They could see chimney smoke rising from Gold Hollow further north.

Charlie pointed out a canyon to the south with a trail down along a creek bed, a safe path to avoid the dangerous town. He went off to help Thatch with the horses.

"It won't be long now," Larson promised Carol. "I've only been there once, but once we're on the flats and pass some homestead ruins, I'll get a fix and recognize the rest of the way. It's actually my uncle's old ranch that he stopped working years ago. He only kept it for a place to hole up in."

"You had an uncle?"

"Black sheep of the family on my mother's side. Hiram Ainsley. He taught me the trade."

She felt admiration. "What else don't I know?"

"He raided for over ten years and was never caught or identified. When he hung it up, he went on a spree. He was shot down last year by a jealous husband in Cheyenne. His sons will be meeting us at the hideout."

"What if they keep the money and don't show up, ever?"

He looked around to make sure the others were out of earshot.

"I lied about them bringing anything." He grinned, pleased with himself. "You see, honey, my cousins think I'm the one who's bringing the loot."

"You mean there's no money for us?" she asked, visibly upset.

"Sure there is. My uncle and I, we stashed it at the hideout all by ourselves with no one else around. It was brand new gold coin. A fortune. And now that my uncle's gone, I'm the only one who knows how to find it, because I'm the only one my uncle trusted."

"But you have to share with your cousins?"

"I needed them to bring us what we need to get to California, and I want them to travel with us in case of Indian trouble, or a posse. But don't worry, honey. There's six of them, all right, but there's plenty of gold to go around. We keep half for ourselves."

"They won't try to take it all?"

"Sweetheart, not everyone is that greedy." He kissed her cheek. "I also decided to let Thatch stick around in case he's needed. He's a better gun then any of them."

"But once they have the gold, why would they need you?"

"I have friends in California that will help them turn it into greenbacks—the gold dust and other coin—so they don't get caught with it, and they won't know who my friends are without me. We won't have any trouble with our half down in South America. They'll love getting real gold down there."

"I'm so tired," she said, her head on his shoulder.

"No worries. Once we meet up on the ranch, you won't have to suffer with a man's saddle anymore. You'll be riding in style."

"Horses were never my—"

"In a wagon, sweetheart. A covered wagon."

"Oh, thank you," she whispered.

She huddled in his arms by the flickering fire as night fell. She longed for a hot bath and clean clothes, a real bed to sleep in, and safe surroundings, even more so as she heard the distant howl of a wolf.

Thatch, wandering nearby but out of earshot of their conversation, grumbled to himself but didn't say out loud he hated Charlie still being with them. He was aware that it was still Larson's intentions to be rid of the Ute, who would soon no longer be needed, but not while Carol was able to see or hear.

On guard over by the horses, Charlie, knowing his life could soon be cut short, raided Larson's stash of gold dust from the pack saddle which had been left with the gear. He left camp before dawn, headed back across the cliffs with the intention of connecting with the posse, mostly because he wanted to be sure Leslie was all right.

In the morning, Larson discovered the missing Charlie and that he was short a bag of gold dust.

"I guess he didn't trust you," Thatch said without revealing his own concerns. To date, Larson had left three of his men in the last mountain range with no trail to follow.

"He would have ended up with a bigger share if he'd stayed," Larson lied, because he still needed Thatch and wanted to impress Carol.

"Not when I got through with him," Thatch muttered as he turned away so Carol could not hear. He envied Larson his lady, but Thatch had not forgotten the one who had gotten away. He had a bump on his head to remind him.

Carol, standing by the fire and huddled in her blankets, was shivering, but Larson gathered her against him in his arms. "Charlie left, but he showed us enough that I can find our trail, so don't worry, honey."

They would soon find their way safely down the canyon and out onto the flats where they stopped at a relay station on the north/south stage road.

After a rest, they continued west on a wagon road through ranch land with cattle and horses grazing on rolling hills. They passed the ruins of homesteads, probably where cattlemen had run off intruders, and Larson knew the rest of the way.

*   *   *   *

It was days later and late evening when the posse made camp near the yellow cliff with a view of the canyons below, the town to the north marked only by chimney smoke, and the valley beyond. It was extremely cold but dry.

Shivering by the campfire, their animals blanketed, they were all weary. Bonnie was the only energy-driven member, always fussing.

"Strange we kept seeing tracks," Finnegan said. "It's almost as if they want us to find them. We might be riding into another ambush."

"Maybe it's my friend Charlie," Leslie suggested.

"Why would he help us?" Finnegan asked.

"He helped me," she countered, unaware that Charlie had started for home but was about to reappear for her benefit.

Kansas had too much on his mind to enter the conversation. Billy was also wrapped in the misery of his own thoughts, pained that his mother would marry Larson so soon after his pa had been murdered.

On guard at first light under a cloudy sky, Billy was half asleep near the fire. He was sitting with his blankets wrapped around him but the cold was keeping him from total sleep.

He looked up and yawned, then gasped.

Charlie stood by the firelight, startling him.

"Hey," Billy said loud enough for the others to waken.

Kansas and Finnegan dropped their blankets and were suddenly their feet with six-guns drawn, but Leslie sat up and waved her hands at them.

"It's my friend, Charlie!" she shouted.

She stood and hurried forward to grasp Charlie's arm and give him a hug as high as she could reach. "Charlie, that's Kansas Red, Mr. Finnegan, and Billy Cassidy."

Charlie tipped his hat as the other men stood in the firelight.

"Charlie, I thought you went home," she said, still gripping his arm.

"I want to tell you the way."

"The way to Larson's hideout?" she asked.

"Yes. I listened to what he said to his woman. I know the place." Charlie then knelt near the fire and traced lines in the dirt as the men came closer.

Bonnie jumped onto the dirt map and scratched on Charlie's leg until he picked her up and let her lick his face. Then he kept her under one arm as he redrew the map.

Charlie showed them how they would bypass Gold Hollow, cross the flats due west, find camping at a grove of cottonwoods by a creek, spot a long ago burned-out homestead, and after several days from there, reach a rocky ridge that half-circled an isolated cabin and barn from the north. There was an open area to the south, which could lead to ambush. He explained they could get down the ridge but would have to lead their horses and take up position in the barn during the night.

"Are you going with us?" Leslie asked as Charlie stood and handed Bonnie to Finnegan,.

"No," he said, accepting a cup of coffee from her.

"So, you're going home to your wife?"

"And son."

"Join us for breakfast, at least?" Finnegan offered.

Wanting to be on his way back east and then north to avoid Larson, Charlie declined. He finished his coffee and turned, aiming for the trees where he had left his horse, but Leslie threw her arms around him one more time.

"You'll always be my friend," she said, releasing him.

Charlie was a bit surprised that Finnegan, Kansas, and Billy came forward to shake his hand. Feeling good about having helped, Charlie tipped his hat and turned away.

They could see him ride from the trees and out of sight, heading northeast.

"He's a good man," Finnegan said. "I know, because Bonnie took up with him really fast."

"Charlie saved my life," Leslie added and turned to sit by the fire once more. She wiped away a tear, sad to know she would likely never see Charlie again.

Each kept to their own thoughts during breakfast. Finnegan missed his ranch and friends and neighbors. He knew his mission was important but it never seemed to end.

Leslie worried over Billy because of Carol and Larson.

Kansas ached with the thought of his past hitting him in the face, and he knew it would not be easy to kill Larson in a fight.

After breaking camp, they rode close to the downhill grade. It was now easier to look out beyond the cliffs and see Gold Hollow's roofs to the north. The safe canyon trail by the creek was also clearly visible to the south.

No one in the posse minded bypassing the town, a well-known trouble spot. They were all ready to catch up with Larson, especially Billy, who could barely contain himself. Finnegan fought to keep a lid on his own feelings, having noticed Kansas's turmoil, along with Billy's grief, and how worried Leslie had become over her companions.

They were soon riding down the steep grade, intending to turn south toward the canyon passage. The sun was high overhead with the first warm day in a week.

They had just reached the creek that led to the canyon trail below when they reined up to stare to the north. At another creek lined with trees, overlooking the trail leading to the roofs of Gold Hollow, a hanging was taking place.

A rope dangled from the barren limb of a cottonwood. Mounted on his sorrel, a young man with a badge on his vest had a noose around his neck. His hands tied behind him, he was sure to die momentarily. If no one interfered.

Surrounding the prisoner were seven rough-looking, heavily-armed men on horseback who were so busy with the kill, they were unaware of the approaching posse. The leader, Paunch, was a big man with great shoulders and a dirty, yellow beard. His cohorts were laughing at the lawman about to die.

Finnegan handed the squirming, growling Bonnie to Leslie. Rifle ready, he waited for Kansas. There was no way they were going to let a lawman hang, but they had to move fast.

Kansas turned to Billy and Leslie. "Cover us."

Leslie and Billy dismounted and moved with their horses, unseen, behind a rocky rise near the trail, their rifles ready for action.

Kansas worked a shell into his rifle's chamber and fired into the air.

The hangmen turned in their saddles to stare as Kansas and Finnegan, his badge showing, rode toward them. Kansas slid his rifle back into the scabbard, making sure his Colt was loose in the holster.

CHAPTER NINE

Paunch, the leader of the seven hangmen, drew his six-gun and turned his horse, as did the others, to watch Kansas and Finnegan approach. "Well, well," he grunted. "Looks like another badge. And a *double* hanging."

Leslie and Billy, covering their friends from high ground, were not seen.

Kansas and Finnegan, no weapons drawn, rode forward at a steady pace until they were some twenty feet away. Paunch held his six-gun on them.

"Join us," the leader said with a sneer. "We got plenty of rope."

"Let him go," Finnegan snapped.

"Not a chance," Paunch growled, waving his six-gun. "He shot my brother."

"You got ten seconds," Kansas said.

After a long moment of suspense, Kansas drew suddenly and they hangmen did not react fast enough. Kansas shot Paunch dead-center as the man yanked on the bridle and set his horse to rearing, starting the mounts behind it. Finnegan also drew as the gang tried to fire back, their horses jumping around under them.

Rifle-fire cracked from the rocky ridge. Two of the seven hangmen jerked and fell from their saddles. And Kansas and Finnegan fired again and again.

In a matter of seconds, the hangmen were all dead on the ground, their horses spinning back from the tree.

The lawman on his quiet sorrel was safe.

A hush followed as Finnegan and Kansas rode among the dead. Then Finnegan pulled a knife and set the lawman's hands free to remove the noose.

"Lucky you got a good horse, or you might have been hanged before we could get to you. But they had to have heard the shots back in town," Finnegan said.

"No worry," the lawman said. "They'll think they're shooting me full of holes for target practice."

They rode away from the hanging tree to where Billy and Leslie appeared, back in the saddle. They could see there was no one coming from the town.

"I'm Finnegan, and this here's Kansas Red."

"Deputy U. S. Marshal Jason Harms."

"Kind of young for the job," Finnegan said, pushing his hat back from his brow.

"I'm twenty-six, but I'll get a lot older, thanks to you fellahs."

"Yeah, but let's move to that next canyon and get out of sight."

Once they were in the canyon, riding along the creek and heading toward the exit to the flats, Finnegan asked the lawman. "What the devil were you doing all by yourself in a place like Gold Hollow?"

"I tracked a killer there, and he resisted arrest, so I shot him."

"So now you're free to help us," Finnegan suggested.

"Help you what?"

"Find Thorn Larson."

Harms shook his head. "You're wasting your time. He's

supposedly under a ton of snow in the Rockies, and when it thaws, they figure they'll find the whole gang under it."

"Larson is less than a week ahead of us," Kansas said.

"You've seen him?"

"She has," Finnegan said, gesturing.

Leslie nodded confirmation.

"Well, right now," Finnegan added, "we'd better high-tail it out of the area before anyone in town gets curious as to why no one's returned yet."

"I don't figure they had any friends," Harms said, "but you're right."

They soon emerged from the safe canyon but hesitated to cross the flats in view of the town. Instead, they chose to ride south for a time, keeping out of sight against the rocky terrain.

At night fall, they camped in a grove of cottonwoods by a shallow stream in the mouth of a secluded canyon. It was a starry night with a bright moon and no wind.

Harms held his coffee cup in both hands and gazed around the fire at his new companions. He liked the surly Kansas and had heard of the bounty hunter. He also enjoyed, the up-front Finnegan, the restless Billy, and the lovely Leslie. He was tickled by Bonnie's sniffing attention and how she jumped up on him to lick his face, then retreated to Finnegan.

Harms also liked the idea of finding Larson, but didn't hold out much hope for it.

"What we're missing, and is a priority," Harms said, "is a gold shipment stolen out of an express office in Pueblo about three years ago. Five- and ten-dollar gold pieces, minted by a company in Denver which is now under ownership of the U.S. Treasury."

They waited for Harms to down his coffee and continue.

"They hit in the middle of the night. A posse tracked them into the Rockies. Later on, they found a string of men shot by their own leader, but one was still barely alive. Before he died, he said their leader was called Hiram and had said he was meeting his nephew at some hideout where they would split the gold."

"And his nephew was Thorn Larson?" Finnegan prompted.

"Yes."

"So that's what Larson meant about gold," Leslie said.

"Assuming we find it," Harms said, "there's a ten-percent reward. That'd be a little over three thousand for each of us, if it's all intact."

For a long moment, they all digested the thought.

"What would you do with yours?" Finnegan asked Harms.

"Settle down and have a bunch of kids," Harms said with a grin. "What about you?"

"I'd restock my own place," Finnegan said, "and I'd ask a certain lady I met on a trip to St. Louis to come out and be my wife."

"I'd put my pa's ranch up for sale, if I'm able," Billy said, "and I'd go somewhere else to start over."

They all looked at Kansas, who was slow to respond.

"I'd stock my ranch in Montana, build it up."

They were surprised that this mysterious gunfighter, a legend in his time, had a ranch anywhere.

Leslie smiled. "I'd buy a herd and ship it to Montana, find a buyer."

Kansas did not meet her gaze. She was too lovely, too smart, too capable, and too much a Texan for him to expect a life with her. He felt her interest but assumed it was in passing and a mere flirtation. It was easier for him to approach it that way than to admit his own attraction for her.

After a time of humor, Finnegan turned to Harms. "They could have spent that money years ago."

"Not one of the coins has showed up in this country."

"So that's why Larson is headed for his old hideout,"

Finnegan said. "He's probably got it hidden there. Maybe planning to leave the country."

"But why wait all this time?" Leslie asked.

"Three years isn't that long," Harms said. "Maybe he and his uncle had some business to clear up, or just wanted to let things cool down about the coins. But we don't know what happened to his uncle either. Hiram could be a first or last name. And he may still be out there."

*   *   *   *

Still days ahead of the posse, Larson, Carol and Thatch, came in view of the rocky ridges circling north of the hideout. Under a clear sky, they rode along a creek lined with cottonwoods, working their way west toward the distant landmark.

"Don't worry," Larson continually said to Carol. He was unaware she was becoming more ill by the hour, shivering under her coat and the blanket wrapped around her.

Sickly from the long journey, she rode wearily at his side, closing her mind to the past, forcing herself to never think back about Sam or Billy or her friends. She concentrated on the new ring on her finger, letting it erase the memory of the one she had thrown away outside the mission.

Larson was offering a life she had always dreamed of, with a mansion, servants, and gowns from Paris, lording it over some new city in South America where they would be the cream of society. They would give tea parties, catered dinners, and an occasional ball to impress their new country.

Larson, himself raised as a gentleman, was ready to take his collected loot and start a new life with the only woman he had ever loved.

Thatch, still hoping to live long enough to get his share,

remained leery and watchful. He had to believe the cousins were bringing the gold.

*   *   *   *

While Larson, Carol, and Thatch traveled west, the newly-formed posse was following their same path.

Deputy Harms and Finnegan were becoming great friends. Bonnie shared them. Kansas, ever the loner, kept to himself, while Billy, still grieving, looked ready to strike out at anyone, except Leslie, who was a calming influence.

One night by the campfire, she saw Billy's stress, and when he got up and walked out in the moonlight, she followed with a blanket around her.

They did not see Kansas in the nearby trees, standing within earshot.

"What can I say to her?" Billy whined to Leslie.

"She's still your mother. You'll always love her, no matter what."

"But she's with Larson. And she has to know he killed my pa."

"We don't know if that's true," Leslie said. "It may have been one of his men."

"Same thing," Billy said, his voice cracking. "I want Larson dead."

"Okay, but it's not up to us. We have a Deputy U.S. Marshal with us."

"Larson won't give up easy," Billy said. "There'll be a fight."

"I know."

"What about you, Leslie? I know how you feel about Kansas."

"He doesn't feel the same."

"Yeah, he's hard as nails, and we don't know that much about him, except for the dime novels, which just make things up."

"Right now, all I can think about is finding your mother."

Billy tugged at his hat brim, dug his left boot toe into the mud, and then shuffled on back to camp. Leslie stood alone, her heart aching for the young man.

She turned, intending to just stare into the night at the stars and moon.

Instead, she found herself facing Kansas, who stood some ten feet away in the trees.

"You startled me," she said, hesitating. "Were you listening?"

He shrugged and walked over but paused several feet from her to look out across the land. Charlie had given good directions, and it wouldn't be long before they were in a fight for their lives.

"Are you really going to Montana?" she asked.

He nodded, avoiding her gaze. "It's time."

"Even if there's no reward?"

Again, he nodded, for he had had enough of his way of life. The only woman he had ever loved had betrayed all those around her, and was now traveling with an outlaw. This young Texas woman before him had shaken him to his boots, but he didn't know what to do about it.

"I've never been to Montana," she said, waiting for an invite.

"It's a place like no other," he responded. "A man can settle down there."

"Alone?"

He didn't take the bait, but he was tempted. He turned and was about to walk around her when she caught his arm and stopped him. He froze as he looked down at her lovely face in the moonlight.

She moved over to him, sliding one hand up around his neck and drawing his head down so that her lips found his. In the cold night, he was burning as if on fire. Her kiss sent lightning strikes through him, from his worn boots to the brim of his hat.

He was helpless, and yet he returned the kiss without holding her, knowing if he did, he'd be lost once and for all.

He drew back a total wreck, met her gaze and the shine in her crystal blue eyes.

"When this is over with Larson," she said, backing away, "let's try that again."

Her sudden, sweet smile was like a hammer on his chest as she turned and walked back toward the fire.

Kansas was completely unhinged and had to walk back into the trees to compose himself. *Lord, is it even possible?*

He knew Larson would put up one heck of a fight. How many in their posse would survive?

* * * *

Another night on the trail across the open land, Larson held Carol close to his side by the firelight.

"All six cousins were named from the Bible," Larson said, "but don't expect them to be saints. Matthew, he'll cut your throat for a shot of whiskey. Mark, he has a dozen notches on his gun. Luke likes to torture. And John is ugly inside and out. Then there's Adam and Abraham—they're from a different mother and somewhat older. They're more peaceable."

Days later, it was late afternoon when Larson, Carol, and Thatch entered the hollow south of the cliffs. To the west, rocky terrain rose high. They saw first the long barn, the corrals with horses, a trough full of rain water, and the covered wagon. Beyond that was a hand-dug well just short of the cabin.

Further back, just beyond the cabin, a four-foot-high rock fence had been started, and stretched some twenty feet toward the barn.

No one had returned to the ranch over some twenty years because the family had died of cholera, and some claimed it was haunted. The barn was missing some of its roof. The cabin had shuttered windows, a wood shed out back, and an outhouse further away. Beyond to the south was a stand of cottonwoods and a creek bed. This place had served as a hideout for him and his uncle, never including gang members, who could talk too much.

To Larson, it was also an escape route to California, just waiting for the right time, and now it was his last ride through. He and his uncle had shared its secrets, but only Larson had survived to visit it once again.

They were greeted at the corral by Larson's cousin Matthew Ainsley, a rather short man in his forties with wiry black beard and beady dark eyes. He had just come out of the barn as they reined up near the board fence. Matthew knew Larson on sight and opened the gate so they could ride inside and dismount.

"Matt, this here's my wife, Carol. And that's Thatch."

Matthew nodded and came to help Carol down.

"Grain the horses," Larson said to Thatch.

"No grain," Matthew said. "We got here a few days ago and found most of the barn roof missing toward the back. Must have happened at least a year ago. Back door was pulled off a hinge and part of that wall is missing. Rain got in pretty heavy and the lid of the grain box leaked like a sieve. It's full of oats all right, but they're all matted and moldy and of no use, except to the mice in there. Even the bin is rotting. There's no hay in the loft, but there's plenty of graze around."

Larson hesitated, then shrugged. "What about the stalls?"

"Up front and dry." Matthew turned back toward the pack horse.

Still, Larson and Thatch walked inside to survey the rain

damage, the missing half of the roof, the dangling back door and a few missing boards on that wall, and then back to the rotting grain bin. He shook his head.

"Must've had a twister."

Thatch spoke in a low voice to Larson. "Where do you think they put the gold?"

Larson shrugged. "We'll find out in time. Don't rush it."

Thatch, agitated, followed Larson back outside.

Meanwhile, Matthew was concentrating on the fact that there was only one pack horse. Unnerved that the one horse could not carry the promised gold along with all the supplies, he figured Larson had better have a good story.

Larson looked toward the cabin and saw smoke coming from the chimney on the south end of it. He walked over to help Carol, for he could see she was wavering.

"We got a fire going," Matthew said. He stayed to help Thatch with the horses but kept his mouth shut about the gold, since he didn't know if he could trust Thatch, who also said nothing.

Larson put his arm around Carol and half-carried her up to the one room cabin. "Come on, honey. We'll get you warm."

The cabin's front door was opened by cousin Luke.

Inside the one-room structure, which had a solid wood floor, there were six cots by the back wall, a table with a total of ten chairs around, and a central back door that led to the woodshed and outhouse. Windows were all around and able to be shuttered. Oil lamps hung on racks near the hearth.

An iron screen stood in front of the hearth where the fire spit and crackled. A coffee pot sat on an iron stand near the flames. A kettle hung by a hook near it.

Larson kept Carol by his side as he introduced them. "Matt, he met us at the corral. That's Luke and John. And Mark. And the two grumpy ones over there, that's Abraham and Adam, the oldest."

Larson's four younger cousins were similar in height and looks. His older cousins, Abraham and Adam, in their fifties, were lighter of skin. Each of the six looked as if they'd cut your heart out.

Carol thought the four younger ones were better-looking and more presentable, even with their black beards needing a trim. The two older cousins looked like they had never had a bath or ever trimmed their scraggly beards.

Matt laid blankets on a chair and put it in front of the hearth. Larson helped Carol sit down, then drew the blankets around her.

"We picked up a bunch of canned food on the way here," Matt said, gesturing to their stacked belongings on one of the cots by the back wall. "We got some soup, Campbell's. On account of Adam, he's missing a lot of teeth from his last bare-knuckle fight."

"Getting a little old for it," Abraham remarked with a toothy grin of his own.

"Soup is good," Larson said, "let's get it out here."

"Yeah, the boys got one of them new fancy can openers," Matt added. "It'll punch it open, but I can do the same with my hunting knife."

"You miss it half the time," John reminded him. "We got the opener because you was gonna slice your leg open the way you were going."

As night fell after sharing soup and canned meats, the cousins gathered around the table to play cards. They had built up the crackling fire in the stone hearth. Coffee steamed near the flames.

Lanterns burned bright where they hung on the walls.

Larson sat with Carol in front of the hearth. Still wrapped in blankets, she looked less feverish and a little stronger. When she fell asleep, Larson got up to see who was winning at cards.

As he approached the table, they stopped playing to glare at him. The six cousins looked angry. Thatch, not sure what was going on, wanted his share of the gold sooner than later and had lost his patience, too.

"All right, where is it?" Matthew blurted at Larson. "There was no gold on your pack horse."

Thatch, seated among them, reacted with his hand on his holster and stared at Matthew and the others. "I thought you all were bringing the gold."

Realizing they had been tricked, all six cousins and Thatch glared angrily at Larson, who, still standing, downed his coffee and acted nonchalant.

"So? Where is it?" Matthew demanded of Larson.

"The gold is on the ranch," Larson replied, addressing his kin. "Your pa and I buried it here three years ago because we dared not spend it at the time. We agreed to wait, but then he got killed, and now it's time to head west."

Relieved, his cousins and Thatch were still chomping at the bit.

"Where is it?" Mark demanded, looking around the room.

"It's not in here," Larson said. "It's buried out there, a long way out, but it stays put until my lady is ready to travel. And you can't find it without me."

It was later that evening that his cousins and Thatch finally calmed down. But all were still silently steaming about the gold. It could be buried in any direction, and they could spend hours digging to no avail, so instead they gritted their teeth and tried to be patient, as they had little choice.

The fire burned bright in the hearth with Carol sleeping close to it in her chair, blanketed and still feverish.

The men sat clustered around the table with the last of the coffee.

"We got the wagon all ready," Mark said. "I hope your friends in California are still there to handle our share of the gold."

"They're a big outfit," Larson said, "so no worry there, and they'll make the switch to greenbacks and other coin without the law ever knowing. But my wife and I will have no trouble with our share in South America."

"We can't hang around here forever," Thatch said. "There could still be a posse out there looking for us."

"Maybe," Larson said, "but we need to travel together for safety, and I want my wife to be a lot better before we move west."

Thatch and Larson's cousins tried not to rile Larson. They had to keep him hale and hearty until they learned the location of the gold.

Matthew got up to stoke the fire and add wood without awakening Carol. He returned to the table and shuffled the cards before addressing Larson.

"You heard about our pa," Matthew said. "Some bartender caught him with his wife and shot him dead, then whacked her behind all the way home."

"I heard," Larson said. "He always had a yen for the ladies."

"We should get some shut-eye," Thatch said, standing with his eye on a cot.

"We're going to flip for the beds," Matthew said. "And somebody's got to be on guard."

"I'll bed down by the fire," Larson said. "I need to keep an eye on my lady."

"She's sure beautiful," Matthew added.

Larson nodded with pride. He had always seen Carol as the most gorgeous woman in the country, and he had despised any competition. When she had married while he was in prison, it had been the worst day of his life.

CHAPTER TEN

M any days later, while Larson, his six cousins, and Thatch waited at the hideout for Carol to recover, the posse rode south across green rolling hills to the high, crimson ridge that half-circled the ranch on the north of it.

It would soon be twilight. They dismounted at the back of the rise and climbed on foot to the brush and rocks at the highest point. They stood behind good cover and could see the cabin far across the open land to the south. It set to the right of the barn and had a woodshed on its west side near an outhouse. Its length ran north to south. Beyond the cabin, they could see cottonwoods and a creek running east to west. They noted the rock fence further back that had not been built more than twenty feet long but was intended to reach the barn.

Several hundred feet away was a larger barn, also with many horses standing in the corrals in front. Between the barn and the cabin, they could see what looked like a hand-dug well surrounded with rock as a frame. A covered wagon was parked closer to the corrals than the cabin.

There was no cover between the ridge and the buildings. It was wide open grassland with only brush and stunted junipers.

Leslie gestured. "See that black horse in the corral with the white markings? That one belongs to Thatch."

"So, they're here, all right," Finnegan said. "And no cover to get there."

A cold south wind was blowing in their faces. The sky was darkening with the coming of twilight, but the moon hung free of the clouds, giving enough light to retain a good view.

"How do we recognize Larson?" Harms asked Leslie.

"Has a big scar, high up, on his left cheek. He always wears a red-and-white striped bandanna. I think Carol gave it to him."

Billy winced and looked away as he wiped at his eyes.

"Let's make camp back in the gully," Harms said. "I figure we should get in the barn a good two hours before sunrise."

Finnegan nodded. "But we'll need to keep an eye on the place, maybe every few hours. Just to be sure they stay put."

"Good idea," Harms said. "But it looks like rain, and I don't figure they'll be in a hurry to move before it clears up."

"I'll stay here awhile," Kansas said.

Deputy Harms, Finnegan, and Leslie were in no hurry to leave the ridge crest, however, because Billy was suddenly acting crazy, pacing and fretting, looking like he was about to explode.

Billy was wild, imagining his mother inside with Larson. He had to put a stop to it.

"I'm going down there," Billy muttered. "Right now."

Kansas glared at him. "You're not going anywhere."

Billy, already a nervous wreck, had had it with the bossy Kansas. "Stop telling me what to do!"

Finnegan started to intervene, then thought better of it. Harms waited to hear what the fuss was all about. Leslie, worried, didn't move. Night was coming on fast. The only light were the stars and moon, often obscured by moving clouds.

"I'm getting my horse," Billy said, about to turn when Kansas stepped in front of him.

"I said no," Kansas snapped.

"Stop trying to boss me," Billy said, his face hot. "My pa was the only one who could ever do that and you have no right."

"Your pa was my brother, and that gives me a right."

"*What?*"

Billy, astounded, stared at Kansas with his mouth open. Leslie, equally amazed, shivered at the revelation. Finnegan just shook his head. Harms waited for more.

Trying to talk back, Billy could not make a sound.

"I'm your Uncle Jack," Kansas said firmly.

It took a long moment before Billy could speak. Kansas was like a rock, a legend, who was human after all—or was he? Billy didn't want to believe him.

"You can't be Jack," Billy snapped. "He died in the war."

"I was in the hospital, but I wasn't dead."

Billy, confused and resistant, finally accepted the claim. "You let my pa think you were? Why?"

"I don't have to answer to you," Kansas said.

"And why not? I'm seventeen, for gosh sakes."

Finnegan gestured to Leslie, who was speechless, and Harms to follow him back down to the horses where they would make camp, leaving Billy and Kansas alone.

Leslie was reluctant, worried, but she left with the others and went down to the campsite.

Uncle and nephew stood alone on the rise under the stars. The moon was slipping into a haze and would soon be covered by clouds.

Billy kept staring at Kansas until his eyes watered. "My pa went through a lot of grief when he saw your name on the list. Why did you let him think you were dead?"

"He was better off without me," Kansas said, staring towards the hideout and the lights in the cabin.

"That wasn't your decision to make," Billy growled,

Kansas turned to look at him in a new light. Maybe the boy had a lot more to him than Kansas had thought. He decided it was time to explain and clear the air, except he could never admit he had left because he couldn't bear to see Carol marry anyone, even his brother. Especially now that he knew what a fool he had been.

"Larson had sworn to kill me, and if I had stayed, your pa would have been a target."

Now it all made sense to Billy, but he was choking on all the information. After a long moment of staring at this strange relative of his, he was finally able to speak.

"My God, you really are my uncle?"

"Yes."

"That's why Pa got so excited when he saw your face on the dime novel," Billy said, suddenly bright and with a flush of joy. "That's why he sent me to find you! Not just because of Larson. So, he knew you were alive after all. I'm glad he knew it before he died."

"So am I."

Kansas held out his hand, and Billy clasped it with a sudden grin.

"Holy cow, I got me an uncle. I got family!" Billy said, ecstatic. "When you go to Montana, can I go with you?"

At Kansas's nod, Billy could hardly handle his joy. "Wowie!"

"I'm hungry," Kansas said, freeing his hand and starting back down.

"Me, too," Billy said with a grin.

Night had fallen as rain clouds hovered.

They walked down, side by side, in the dark. Kansas had his

own thoughts on family, sharing Billy's joy after so many years. He liked the youth, but it was still painful to think of the years he had wasted, being alone instead of with his brother, whatever the reasons.

They reached the others, who had built a fire in a dug-pit, setting up a tarp to protect it and them from the sprinkles now turning into rain. Their only light came from the crackling flames. They had hot coffee and beans. Finnegan and Harms did not question Billy and Kansas, but Leslie could hardly keep from it.

The two men, uncle and nephew, sat side by side and often smiled at each other.

"Billy," she said, "I've not seen you this happy in a long time."

"I got family," Billy said, grinning at Kansas.

Bonnie seemed to like Billy's demeanor but landed in Kansas's lap.

"We'd better get to sleep early," Harms offered. "We want to be in that barn a good hour before sunup."

Leslie was glad for Billy, but she knew he still had to deal with his mother having married Larson. She also saw Kansas in a new light, and she liked what she saw.

Much later that night with the rain gone and stars returning with the moonlight, Kansas took another turn at watch up on the ridge, replacing Finnegan. Wearing a heavy coat, he settled on a rock with a cup of coffee in his hand. He did not move nor turn when Leslie joined him, but he knew she was there because he had seen her start up the ridge.

She had a blanket wrapped around her. It was now bitter cold.

Under the starry sky with its occasional drifting clouds and the silvery moon, they sat in silence for a time. They could see lamp lights in the cabin and felt sure no one was leaving the hideout anytime soon. Finally, Leslie spoke softly.

"You made Billy very happy," she said. "And me, too."

He looked at her with a silent question.

"Because it's nice to know you're human," she said with a smile.

He thought of that first time he'd seen her, of carrying her in his arms when they had found her injured. He realized he had already been on his way to falling for her. He remembered their one-time embrace, and then of the unexpected kiss that had nearly disabled him. He sipped his coffee to keep his calm. He had already included Billy in his life. A breathtaking, feisty woman would be much more difficult. And why would she even be interested? He had never wanted anything more for himself than to be with her, but he was worried it might be too late for him.

She shivered. "But I have to ask, why did you never return to your family?"

"I'm the reason Larson went to prison and ended up on posters. He was sworn to kill me, and I didn't want my brother to end up a target."

He frowned, thinking of the price his brother had paid, just the same.

He was also conscious of Leslie's nearness and how sweet it would be to reach out and take her in his arms. Yet he couldn't move. They were silent a while longer, staring at the cabin, before she spoke again.

"When this is over," she said, "you're going to Montana?"

Kansas nodded without looking at her.

"Is Billy going with you?" she persisted.

"Yes."

"Maybe I'll ride along," she offered.

He nodded assent but could not say what was on his mind, how he could see the three of them finding a new life in the north country, and yet knowing they may not live through the coming fight.

"It's not over for Billy," she said after a time. "Seeing his mother with Larson may be more than he can handle. Especially if Larson is his father."

He nodded and kept his eyes on the hideout.

"So I'm glad he has you," she added, then shook her head. "Jack Cassidy. That will take getting used to."

He downed his coffee and she held her hand out to take the cup. He nodded thanks.

She smiled and drew her blanket tighter against the cold before heading back down to camp. Kansas had to collect himself, for if it were ever possible, he knew now there was no other woman he would rather have by his side than Leslie.

But there had been another time when, as a student of the ministry, he had hidden in the trees across from the church with his mount and pack horse and watched the beautiful Carol wed his older brother, Sam.

Once he'd learned he had been put on the casualty list, he'd taken that as a sign.

First he had found work as a hired gun, then a bounty hunter, and sometimes, a lawman. He'd fallen into a somber existence, a sanctuary, a place where he could be without looking back.

Now, after all the revelations and painful truth, he found he was grateful that Leslie had stirred emotions he thought he would never have again.

He felt there was hope for him, after all.

But only if they survived the ugly confrontation to come.

Down at the campsite, while Finnegan and Harms slept near the fire, Leslie came with her blankets to where Billy sat awake on the other side of it. She huddled next to him. They spoke quietly.

"I can't believe it," he whispered.

"I'm glad for you, Billy."

"He was a bounty hunter. A gunfighter. Why?"

"Maybe he was good at it, and bringing in the bad guys, that's not a bad thing."

"No, I guess not."

"When this is over, you'll be on his ranch in Montana."

"Are you coming with us?"

"I would like to."

"I seen how he looks at you. He likes you a lot."

She smiled and snuggled into her blankets. "I like him, but we need to get some sleep, Billy. We're facing a big fight tomorrow."

"I hope Ma doesn't get hurt," he muttered. "No matter what she's done, she's still my mother."

"Billy, I think you're all grown up."

He smiled at her praise and drew his blankets up to his nose. He closed his eyes, but the realization that he had an uncle in his life woke him up now and then.

*   *   *   *

Two hours before sunrise, the posse rode across the open land. They could see lights burning low in the cabin and thin smoke swirling from the chimney.

Inside the barn, they dismounted and put their horses in the empty stalls under the remaining northern half of the roof. Moonlight cast a glow from above. They could see missing boards on the back wall where the door hung on one hinge.

Finnegan set Bonnie down in the straw while he checked the grain bin. He lit a match to look inside the rotting container.

"It's gone bad. Moldy," he said to the others, "and lots of mice droppings."

He put out the match and let the lid close haphazardly.

"Good thing we still have some with us," Harms said.

Bonnie immediately attacked the rotting, outside bottom of the bin. She whined and dug frantically at the scent of the mice coming from inside.

"That'll keep her busy," Finnegan said with a grin. "She loves to chase a mouse, and from what I saw in there, she won't soon run out of 'em."

Up front, Billy kept looking out a partially-shuttered front window of the barn facing the cabin. Tormented by the knowledge that his mother was with Larson, Billy was yet of lighter heart because his uncle, Jack Cassidy, was there, alive.

Kansas was at the front sliding door of the barn, briefly stepping out to look past the wagon at the north edge of the cabin. He stood quietly as the outlaws' horses in the corral mainly slumbered and ignored the visitors.

Leslie was at the back of the barn, finding a rear window with a view of the cabin, and sliding the shutter only slightly open. She could see the partially-built, twenty-foot-long rock fence to her left, and the cottonwoods further back.

Harms and Finnegan were at a center window looking across at the front door of the cabin. Lights were pale inside, indicating lamps now burned low while the intruders slept. Smoke was all the more thin from the chimney, another sign they were asleep and not tending the fire.

"They're pretty confident," Finnegan said.

"At first light," Harms said, "I'll give 'em the word."

"Let's make it easy for you," Finnegan replied, hunting through a pile of trash and cans near the grain bin where Bonnie was still busy. He found a large tin can and set about making a hole in the bottom of it with his knife.

* *

An hour later in the cabin, just before sunup, Larson was awake and stoking the fire, then adding another chunk of wood. Coffee steamed in the hearth with hot coals under its iron rack.

Carol was still asleep in a chair in front of the fire, covered with blankets. He bent over to feel her cold brow and worried.

He didn't like the fact it was so smoky inside the cabin.

Unaware he was being watched, Larson opened the front door and looked around, allowing fresh air in from the cold night. It was nearly dawn, and he had yet to deal with his cousins, Thatch, and the gold. Easily identified by his striped bandanna, he paused to look again at the starry sky.

Billy nearly climbed out the barn window as he agonized until Larson went back into the cabin, closing the door behind him. Finnegan joined Billy to keep him under control.

Still standing at the central window, Harms had a good view as well. Leslie, at the rear window, worked a shell into the chamber of her repeater.

At the front door of the barn, Kansas could step out just far enough to see the first window of the cabin. He backed away and kept just inside, his rifle ready.

Bonnie continued to chew away at the rotting bottom of the bin. She could smell the mice inside and was determined to get every one of them, even if she had no plan as to what she would do with even one, except to give it a good shaking. Now, hearing a squeak inside, she had new energy and whined as she dug.

Finnegan turned from Billy to grin at her, and then was back at the window.

Kansas walked back into the barn as the others had a better view of the cabin. He found himself joining Leslie at the rear, partially-shuttered window.

"Counting the saddle horses," she said, "there must be at least nine people in there, including Carol. I know he has a lot of cousins. And Thatch is still with him, I think."

Kansas agreed with her estimate and nodded.

"It will hurt Billy, seeing her with Larson," she said softly. "And it's really going to hurt if it turns out Larson's his father. I hope it isn't true. And I pray he never finds out, if it is."

Kansas nodded agreement again.

"But he has you now," she said. "And he's really proud of it."

They heard a sudden growl as Bonnie's gnawing at the bottom of the bin sent a squeaking mouse charging into nearby straw. Bonnie leaped after it, but the little mouse had an escape route and she lost the scent.

Back to the bottom of the bin, Bonnie continued scratching and chewing. Kansas had to grin at the little dog as he headed back to the front door.

Within the hour, it was first light. Any minute now, someone might come out to check on the horses.

Harms took the tin megaphone, stood next to an open window, and shouted loud and clear.

"You in the cabin! This is U.S. Deputy Marshal Harms! With a posse! Come out with your hands up!"

Inside the cabin, the six cousins and Thatch all jumped to the windows and slid the shutters aside to peer at the barn. They saw no one as they hunched down. Larson turned Carol's chair and lifted her in his arms, awakening her. He lay her down near the fire as she stared up at him. He stayed at her side.

"Stay down, honey."

Harms yelled again. "Drop your guns and come out! Hands up!"

Matthew slid over to Larson. "We'll get out the back and get behind the barn."

155

Larson nodded his assent. Matthew, Mark, and Luke slipped out the back door and moved to the south side of the cabin, crouching down, hoping they wouldn't be seen. They were planning to make it to the partially-built rock fence at the back of the barn.

Abraham and Adam followed them out the back door but moved toward the north side of the cabin to slip around toward the front and head for the wagon as cover.

Cousin John stayed inside, near the front window close to the hearth. He moved the shutter partly aside.

Thatch hunkered down near Larson, who knelt at Carol's side. "You'd better tell us where the gold is. If they get you, we'll be out of luck."

"Then you'd better make sure I stay alive," Larson snapped

From the barn, Harms yelled again through the tin can. "You got three minutes before we blow that cabin apart."

Finnegan, Billy, and Harms had their rifles at cracks in the barn wall, avoiding the obvious windows. Leslie was finding rifle slot openings near the back. She had another idea and headed for the front of the barn.

Kansas, peering out the front door, saw no cover between him and the wagon except the corral fence. Suddenly, Leslie was at his side.

"They won't shoot me," she said. "Let me go talk to them and see if I can get Carol out of there."

"No."

"What? You're not the boss here!"

"I'm your boss."

"That'll be the day," she snapped, even as she saw the humor in his eyes.

"Just get back."

She glowered at him but hid her smile as she turned away.

As she headed to the rear window facing the cabin, Finnegan called softly to her from the central window.

"Watch it. Three of 'em just ducked behind that rock fence. I'll try and get 'em from here."

Harms moved to the forward side window to replace Billy, who joined Kansas up front.

They could not see Abraham and Adam because the wagon blocked their view.

"Stay here," Kansas whispered to Billy and headed back inside.

At the rear window, Leslie spotted Matthew on a run from behind the rock fence, heading toward the back of the barn. She fired and Matthew stumbled backwards, firing his pistol in the air as he fell dead. Mark, behind the fence, raised up to return Leslie's fire.

Finnegan shot Mark twice as the man spun around and fell.

Luke, hunched down, had taken advantage of the shooting to hurry around the cabin and run in through the back door.

"They got an army out there!" Luke said, out of breath as he joined Thatch and Larson near the front windows.

Carol awakened and called out. "Thorn?"

Keeping down, Larson hunched over and got to her. He knelt to kiss her hand. "Stay down on the floor, honey."

Leaving her with the chair down in front of her as some protection, Larson went back to where Thatch waited by the far window on the other side of the front door. John and Luke were at the window near the hearth.

Knowing Abraham and Adam were out there, they waited for signs before laying a barrage on the barn.

Billy, peering out the front doors of the barn, saw feet behind the wagon as Abraham and Adam crept near it. He waited until they started a run for the corral fence, not knowing he was there.

Billy shot Abraham, who was hit in the shoulder and dove back behind the wagon.

Adam sought cover, but as Kansas hurried to join Billy, he spotted Adam moving toward Abraham and fired. Adam jerked, fell backward and died. Furious, Abraham crept out to take a shot at Kansas, who fired again and hit him dead-center.

Kansas returned to Billy's side just inside the door.

"How many more men do you think are in that cabin?" Billy asked, frustrated.

"We know Larson's in there, and his man, Thatch. We saw one break from the rock fence and get back inside. I don't know what others are there."

"I hope my mother stays down on the floor," Billy said, worried sick.

"I'm sure of it," Kansas said, but didn't say Larson would be protecting her.

Inside the cabin, where Carol still huddled on the floor by the hearth, Luke and John peered out the front window nearby.

"They got Adam and Abraham by the wagon," Thatch said as he looked out the window near the north side of the cabin.

Angry, John rose up to fire out the window and was suddenly hit in the upper chest by Finnegan's rifle. Wounded, he dropped and rolled in pain.

Furious, Luke took John's place, saw someone at a barn window and raised up to fire, just as his target, Harms, fired back and hit him in the face. Luke spun away from the wall, staggering about until he hit the floor and rolled over, dead.

Terrified, Carol squealed and shriveled up in her blankets.

Larson, the wounded John, and Thatch were the only survivors, except for Carol.

"Now what?" Larson muttered, furious.

Thatch reloaded. "I'm going out to the creek bed and work my way around behind the barn. They won't see me, and there's a big opening in the back wall. I'll get as many as I can."

Thatch took the dead Luke's six-gun and reloaded it. Now with two loaded weapons, one in his belt and one in his right hand, he was going to kill a lot of the posse, maybe all.

"First, you got to tell me where the gold is," Thatch growled.

Larson quickly lied. "It's in the well."

Thatch snickered with delight and headed out the back door.

While Larson kept firing at the barn, and the wounded John lay bleeding, Thatch slipped away out of sight, past the outhouse, unseen by the posse in the barn. He made it to the creek bed which was lined with cottonwoods. The water was low in what was a deep ditch. He crouched down and moved quickly until he was east of the barn before creeping up to it, out of sight. He headed for the missing boards and was at the back of the barn with a six-gun in each hand. He slipped through the opening and saw Leslie with her back to him at the rear window.

Kansas had moved to be with Billy up front by the sliding door. Finnegan and Harm were firing from forward windows with their backs to Leslie and the intruder.

Thatch sneered. She was the one who had got away. Maybe he would shoot the lawman and then grab her for the finish. First he had to hit her on the head with his pistol to put her out, so he started sneaking toward her.

At the same second, Bonnie had chased a mouse from the bin toward the back and saw Thatch. She jumped, barked crazily, and ran to attack his boots.

Startled, Thatch tried to kick the dog away.

Leslie spun, saw him and fired her rifle, hitting Thatch in the chest.

Startled, amazed, Thatch could not believe she had shot him.

She worked another shell in the chamber but he slowly fell, staring at her and dying before he hit the dirt. Leslie backed away at the horrid sight.

Bonnie lost interest when he fell and returned to the bin.

Harms came to see if she was all right, then went back to the center window.

Finnegan remained at the forward window, while Billy and Kansas were at the sliding door.

Meanwhile, the barrage from the barn was keeping Larson so busy at the rear window, he didn't know what Thatch was doing in the barn. He also didn't heed that John was still alive and gripping his pistol, dazed and close to death where he had crawled to the wall near the hearth.

At the same time, Larson heard Carol sobbing. Afraid she was hit, he panicked and quickly rose up to go to her. A shot through the window hit him in the center of his upper back. He staggered forward, aghast, and reached the wall near the back door. He turned crazily and sat down with a thud, his back against the wall with gun in hand, staring at the closed front door.

Gunfire abruptly halted from the barn.

Carol staggered to her feet and around her chair, leaving her blankets, and stumbled over to Larson's side. She knelt and tearfully put her hand to his face. He smiled with blood on his lips and was barely alive.

At the barn, Kansas had joined Leslie where Thatch lay dead. Harms and Finnegan had stopped their barrage with no return fire and turned for a look.

Bonnie was still whining and digging under the bin.

At the front door of the barn, Billy reloaded his pistol. He could wait no longer and charged across the open ground. The others watched him through the window and were frantic.

Billy threw the cabin door open and stared across the room where his mother knelt at the side of the badly wounded Larson, who was still propped up against the back wall. Billy hardly noticed that the dying John was rising on his elbow with six-gun in hand.

Larson looked strangely at the angry young man who aimed down at him while standing framed in the open doorway.

"You killed my pa," Billy said fiercely. "Now it's your turn."

"No!" Carol cried, half shielding the dying outlaw. "Thorn is your father!"

Billy gasped, stood frozen, horrified, unable to pull the trigger.

Behind Billy, who still blocked the doorway, Kansas had heard and made ready to catch the youth if he needed it. Leslie came in close behind Kansas for the same reason.

Larson tried to speak to the son he had never seen until this moment. His lips moved and blood ran down his chin. He was not going to say he wanted to claim Billy. He only wanted to tell the boy he was lucky Thorn Larson was his father.

Billy, shocked and ashamed, still felt the urge to end this terrible man's life.

Carol, frantic, rose on one knee as if to go to Billy, not knowing how to handle his pain but determined to save Larson.

Still aiming at Larson, Billy caught a glimpse of movement to his left.

John had lifted his pistol to fire at Billy, who spun and fired first, hitting John dead-center. John's shot then went wild as he jerked around and pulled the trigger while dying. The stray bullet hit Carol in the right side of her head as she tried to rise.

Wide-eyed, she fell back, cried out, and dropped beside the dying Larson as he tried to reach for her.

Billy froze, unable to draw back the hammer, and dropped to his knees.

Larson saw Kansas in the doorway behind Billy, but didn't recognize him.

Billy turned, looked up, then spoke clearly to Larson. "Meet my Uncle Jack."

Larson, furious to learn Jack Cassidy was alive, tried to raise his pistol but could not. Then the outlaw slowly closed his eyes and died with a dead Carol at his side.

All in the room still alive felt the impact of the painful truth.

Billy stood and swayed, so badly shaken he could barely holster his weapon. Kansas took him by the elbow and turned him outside as Finnegan and Harms passed them to join Leslie.

Kansas led Billy over to the well so the boy could lean on the rock frame of it.

"I don't care what he said," Billy said in great agony. "My real father was Sam Cassidy, the best man I ever knew."

"He was, and you're doing him proud," Kansas said, hurting for his nephew and himself.

CHAPTER ELEVEN

After the burials, and some house cleaning, it was twilight when the posse finally rested up in the cabin. They opened the canned meats and soups they had bought at Donovan's. Leslie made more coffee, and after supper, they all remained at the table with their cups. They were exhausted.

Each of them had their own thoughts about the raid, but they knew Billy had the most turmoil. Kansas didn't share his own pain and was ready to run outside to be alone.

"What about Bonnie?" Harms asked. "When we let her back outside, she took off for the barn again."

"She won't stop chewing up that bin until she gets a mouse," Finnegan said with a grin. "Then she'll give it to someone as a gift."

"I'll check on her," Kansas said. "And the horses."

Ready to get out of the room and clear his thoughts, Kansas stood up.

"Okay," Finnegan said, "but take her some of that leftover beef, will you?"

Kansas went to the hearth to collect a bit of the beef from the still-hot pan and put it on a small plate. He could hardly wait to escape to some solitude. He knew what Billy was going through, but he also had an ache to work out of his own system.

Kansas went outside with the beef, while Harms and Finnegan stretched out on cots and were soon fast asleep.

Leslie and Billy moved to chairs in front of the fire where they could finish their coffee and not be easily heard. The fire was well-stoked. They spoke softly.

"None of it's your fault, Billy."

"Maybe it wasn't hers either," Billy said. "But a set of circumstances don't make him my real father."

"No, it doesn't," Leslie said softly.

"Larson was nothing to me," Billy said. "My real pa was Sam Cassidy, and he's the best man I ever knew. He was kind, smart, working to make me grow up a better person. He never had a bad word to say about anyone. He must have known all along how I came about, but I was his son, all the way. He knew the truth, but he loved my mother just as she was, so I got to do the same. And I'm going to be just like him."

"You already are," she said.

"And I got me an uncle, so don't let him get away."

"You think?"

"The three of us, we got to go to Montana. So go get him, okay?"

She shared a smile with him. "On my way."

She pulled on her coat and went outside in the moonlight.

At the barn, she found that Kansas had lit a lamp which hung on the wall nearby. He was watching Bonnie frantically dig around the rotting grain bin. He had given her the beef, which had been cleaned off the plate still on the straw, but the little dog was not about to let the mice get away.

Kansas, standing with his back to Leslie, having seen her

coming from the cabin, pretended to barely notice her as he spoke, referring to Bonnie, sort of.

"Some females don't know how to give up."

"Lucky you," Leslie said.

"Meaning?"

He refused to look at her as he watched Bonnie's losing another mouse, the tiny rodent dashing under old straw. Bonnie didn't bother to chase it but returned to the bin, which seemed to harbor a whole family of mice. One squeaked inside of it. Bonnie kept digging at the base of it and whining.

Leslie moved up behind Kansas, who still would not turn.

"I want six children," she said, "and a dozen grandchildren."

"Why tell me?"

"Because we're getting married."

"I don't remember asking you."

"We don't waste time in Texas."

She took his left arm and turned him to face her. He held his breath and fought back a smile as he looked down at this incredibly beautiful woman. She could be a new life, a whole new world, and his only chance at a happy future. He felt the pain in his heart was turning into joy. He realized he had loved her from the moment of her rescue when he had held her in his arms. And the more she had badgered him, the more he had wanted to be with her.

He tried to look grim but he knew he was a goner.

She slid into his arms and pulled his head down to kiss him firmly.

Kansas nearly collapsed as he hugged her to him and kissed her passionately.

They continued to embrace and kiss until Bonnie suddenly barked shrilly behind them.

Turning while still wrapped together, they looked down to

see Bonnie had become even more frantic. Then they saw the collapsed side of the bin, and gold coin spilling out right and left. Five- and ten-dollar pieces, brand new, uncirculated gold.

"My God," Leslie said with a giggle.

"Go get the marshal," he responded with a big grin.

She moved from his arms and could not stop laughing as she made her way to the cabin.

Inside, she called out loud. "Heads up!"

Billy, half asleep by the fire, looked up. "What?"

Finnegan and Harms, startled awake, sat up on the cots and rubbed their eyes.

"Bonnie found the gold. In the barn."

"Wowie!" Billy said.

Leslie turned and ran back out in the moonlight. She rejoined Kansas, who put his arm around her as they watched Bonnie scattering the gold pieces as she dug.

Billy, Harms, and Finnegan soon appeared, and stopped to stare at the growing pile of gold.

"Holy cow," Billy said.

"They must've put in a false bottom," Harms said with a grin.

Finnegan knelt to pick up some of the coins and handed them to Harms.

"We'll have to dig it out and do a count," Harms said. "We can take the rewards out for finding the gold before we move the rest of it, and Finnegan can help me get it home. Then we'll send you a share of the reward for Larson. Send me an address at the marshal's office in Denver."

"Wow," Billy said. "We can buy a lot of beef with that."

"You bet," Kansas said, hugging Leslie to his side.

Billy grinned as he realized Leslie had his uncle in tow.

Bonnie squirmed as Finnegan picked her up. "You've done your job, Bonnie. Time to rest up."

Billy was dancing around.

"Here, hold her," Finnegan said, shoving Bonnie into Billy's arms.

Billy panicked but Bonnie hurriedly licked his face as if she had waited a lifetime to get at him. She had mouse-breath and he made a face but petted her happily.

"Let's get those buckets over there," Harms said.

Later inside the cabin by lamplight, with stacks of coins on the table, Harms had them all sign a piece of paper with the count and distribution. Each person had a huge reward of three thousand dollars in front of them.

They paused a long moment to catch their breath and enjoy the magnitude of it.

"Wow, Uncle Jack, we'll own half of Montana!" Billy said. "We can buy a lot of really fine horses with this."

"And build a barn," Leslie said. "But there's something that comes first, before we ever get there."

She gave Kansas a stern look and he grinned.

"We can stop in Salt Lake City," Kansas told her. "And find a priest. Billy can be my best man."

Billy grinned from ear to ear.

"If you want to sell your ranch," Finnegan said to Billy, "the marshal here can help me write up a paper you can sign, and then I can handle it for you. And you can let me know when you get settled in Montana."

Two days later, Finnegan, Bonnie, and Harms, with pack horses in tow, were on their way east, leading several outlaw horses that were able to travel.

Billy, Leslie, and Kansas took the covered wagon west into Utah Territory, and then north where they found themselves in awe of a land of red, yellow, and white bluffs in amazing shapes, with snow bright against waves of crimson heights.

Kansas remained reserved emotionally, but Leslie was patient, and believed herself a winner when they reached Salt Lake City. They were married in a chapel after a long wait, because Leslie had insisted on a white wedding gown by way of a local seamstress.

When she walked into the chapel and up the aisle with Billy, Kansas was speechless. The tough, sharpshooting Texan had turned into an angel, with white flowers in her flaxen hair hanging down to her waist, and with a long flowing veil and roses in her cheeks.

Kansas was done for and so was his heart.

Weeks later, the wagon rolled onto a rise overlooking a fertile valley with sparkling streams, dark pines and quivering aspens up to the snow capped mountains. Elk roamed the meadows.

The shack still in place would one day be a long, rambling ranchhouse.

Prize horses and beef cattle would roam the valley.

Children would be chasing their Uncle Billy.

And Kansas and Leslie would be sitting on the porch in the shade, counting their blessings.

ABOUT THE AUTHOR

Western novelist and screenwriter **Lee Martin** grew up on cattle ranches in Northern California. Martin began writing in the third grade and, later in life, wrote and sold 43 short stories before turning to novels, with *The Desperate Riders* the 28th now published, and with three screenplays now produced.

The novel is now a motion picture. *The Desperate Riders*, written by Lee Martin, produced and directed by Michael Feifer in Tennessee, was released February 25, 2022, to select theaters as well as online streaming and TV on demand. The DVD will be released in April, 2022. Stars include Drew Waters, Trace Adkins, Tom Berenger, Vanessa Evigan, Sam Ashby, Victoria Pratt, Cowboy Troy, Rob Mayes, Brock O'Hurn and Peter Sherayko.

Martin's novel *The Siege at Rhyker's Station*, with a screenplay by Lee Martin, was filmed in the mountains of Southern California in November of 2020, It was released in December of 2021 as *Last Shoot Out*, produced and directed by Michael Feifer, and stars Brock Harris, Skylar Witte, Peter Sherayko, Jay Pickett, David Deluise, Michael Welch, Brock Burnett, Caia Coley, Keikilani Grune, Cam Gigandet, and the legendary Bruce Dern. It received a great review in Variety. And Martin has just been awarded a Spur Award by Western Writers of America for the screenplay.

Martin left the practice of law to write full-time, primarily concentrating on Western screenplays and novels, and often converting one to the other. Martin's screenplay for **Shadow on the Mesa**, starring Kevin Sorbo, Wes Brown, and Gail O'Grady, was based on Martin's novel of the same title (Five Star Publishing, 2014). The movie was the second-highest-rated and second-most-watched original movie in Hallmark Movie Channel's history when it premiered in 2013. The film also won the prestigious Wrangler Award given by the National Cowboy & Heritage Museum in Oklahoma City for Best Original TV Western Movie.

Martin's novels, **The Grant Conspiracy**, **The Last Wild Ride**, and **Fury at Cross Creek**, all received rave reviews from *True West Magazine* and were also written as screenplays, as is **Fast Ride to Boot Hill**. **In Mysterious Ways**, Martin's new modern suspense Western, received great critical acclaim from *Kirkus Reviews* and *Midwest Book Reviews*.

Hang Town, one of Martin's most recent novels, now also optioned for the script version, received a fine review from *Roundup Magazine*: "Lee Martin gives the reader a plot and a cast of characters ready-made for a riveting teleplay. Action, romance, and revelation appear on every page."

Martin is always working on the next novel and screenplay. For the latest news, follow Lee Martin Westerns on Facebook.